Planet

of

Shadows

Books
by
R. J. F.

<u>Tales of the Multiverse</u>
Book 1: Monster versus Mortal
Book 2: Sarah
Book 3: Scar
Book 4: Planet of Shadows
Book 5: The Mysterious Four

<u>Darphopia</u>
Darphopia: The Godless Land
Darphopia: The Godless Land Collector's Edition
Darphopia: The Second God War
Darphopia: The Second God War Collector's Edition

<u>R. J. F. Shorts</u>
The Seducter (e-book only)
The Council of Cats (e-book only)

<u>Gamebooks</u>
Pencilventure: The Ancient Forest Temple

Planet

of

Shadows

R. J. F.

Dedicated to Gran Gran and Grumps, who have always supported my work from the very beginning.

Chapter 1

The school bell chimed throughout the building, signalling to every high school student that it was time to enter the warzone we called a hallway. We all stood from our desks, grabbed our books, and started for our next classes. But before anyone had managed to leave the classroom, Mr. Burns, our teacher, had a few final words. "Remember, class, there's a history assignment next week, and I strongly suggest you all study for it."

As usual, we continued walking as if we hadn't heard what he said. Mr. Burns had tried to threaten us with our bad test scores before, saying how we all needed to shape up if we didn't want to fail his class, but I honestly don't think half the school cares.

Books in hand, I entered the hallway and witnessed the horrors: people skateboarding up and down the halls, people throwing footballs around like bullets, people making out in secluded areas (and also right out in the open, right in front of their jealous exes, begging to start up a violent love triangle), people stealing lunch money, people earning lunch money by selling drugs and test answers, people stuffing smaller kids into lockers, and everything was topped off with that strange concoction of smells high schoolers emit that makes it hard to tell the marijuana users from the harsh cologne users.

I try to stay out of all that. I wouldn't want to be one of the kids getting stuffed into a locker. I'm an average-sized guy, but I wouldn't stake that against someone's ability to get me to fit in one of those things, especially given how unpopular I am.

Suddenly, a football came flying toward me, and I ducked out of the way, right into two bulky guys who pushed me off of them and onto the floor. I dropped all my books.

"Watch it!" one of them said. "Your pasty ass almost sprained my arm."

"Don't look too long," said the other guy. "I hear blond blinds."

They left, laughing to each other. That was par for the course, getting made fun of for how I look with jokes that barely made any sense.

I tried to gather my books quickly, but it was hard when countless people were bumping into me and stepping all over my stuff. One girl even went as far as to throw an eraser at my head.

"Hey!" I looked up at her.

"What?" she challenged.

"Uh, nothing." I put my head down. She had muscles and a nose piercing; no way I could handle that.

"Exactly. Your fat head's in my way."

"Sorry."

She spat next to me and then left.

You can really tell a school sucks when the teachers don't even notice all this stuff happening ... or maybe they don't care.

My last book was picked up off the ground, not by me, by a girl with short, chestnut-brown hair. She handed me the book with one hand and held her own books with the other. After I took my book from her, she helped me up.

"Thanks," I muttered cautiously.

I started down the hallway with my head down, but she followed me.

"So what's your name?" she asked.

I looked up at her. She was smiling. "Are you talking to me?"

"Who else would I be talking to?"

"I don't know, someone like ..."

"Like those bullies who always pick on you? I think they have enough attention. You should stand up for yourself. Don't take their crap."

I sighed. "Can't."

"Why not?"

"Because they'd just beat me up anyway. I'd rather just stay out of it." I sighed again.

She was looking at me, but I couldn't tell what she was thinking. I'm not very good at that. "You didn't answer my first question," she said.

"First question?"

"Your name?" she restated.

"Oh, right, sorry. It's Charles. What's, um, yours?"

"Angela." She grinned. "What class are you heading to?"

"Math."

"Who with?"

"Mr. Turner."

She made a weird face. "I have him for geography. He *sucks*."

"He's not that bad, just strict."

"Are you kidding? One time, I swear he stifled a laugh because I forgot how many continents there are."

I smirked.

"Oh, come on. Who actually remembers Australia counts as a continent?"

"I do."

"Okay, well, maybe not everyone's as smart as you." That could have been an insult, but she said it like how my sister says it, and she never means it offensively.

We turned a corner.

"So ... do you like movies?" she asked.

"Yeah, I guess."

"Would you want to see one some time? Together? Maybe on Friday?"

I looked at her.

"Or ... another day."

I couldn't believe it. Not only was she actually talking to me, but she wanted to hang out with me outside of school. Weird. "Sure, I guess that could be fun. I don't know what day, though. I'll have to check."

"Okay, cool. Give me your phone."

"Why?"

"So I can put my number in." She had her hand out.

I pulled my phone out of my pocket and gave it to her, and she tapped in her number and then gave it back to me. "There. Just text me when you know." She smiled, and her cheeks were a little red. "I think I missed my turn. I'll see you later." She hurried off in the opposite direction.

I stared at her number on my phone. She put herself down as "Ange" with a heart emoji next to her name. I couldn't tell if that meant something. People do that, right? That's a self-expression thing. I couldn't tell what she was expressing, though.

When I reached my math class, Mr. Turner was standing outside, yelling at one of his students.

"Tardiness is not an acceptable trait, Mr. Mathews," he said.

"I'm sorry. Won't happen again."

Mr. Turner looked at me. "Mr. McCoy, do you know what time it is?"

"Uh, no," I answered. "Don't you have a clock in the classroom, though? You can just check that."

The other student smirked for some reason.

Mr. Turner crossed his arms. "Don't be flippant with me, Mr. McCoy. You're late. Both of you, get to class."

How was I being flippant? He asked me for the time, didn't he? Or did he not mean that?

I entered the classroom with the other student and approached the second-row desk on the leftmost side of the room, where I usually sit. It was occupied by some girl, one who always hangs around all the guys who like to bully me.

"Excuse me," I said.

"What?" She scowled, not even bothering to look at me.

"That's my spot."

"So?"

"I always sit there."

"I don't see your name on it."

"But that's my spot."

"Oh, my god, man, just sit somewhere else." She glared at me. "What sort of freak show has a special spot? Touch grass, man."

I don't even know what that means.

"Move." I was pushed out of the way by another one of my many bullies.

"Hey, you," the girl said to him.

"'Sup, Abi?" He smiled at her.

"Saved you a seat."

"Hell yeah." He sat at the desk next to her.

The girl looked at me and then back to the guy. "Xavier, get this. I'm sitting in this guy's 'special spot.'"

He looked at me and laughed. "Who has a special spot? What are you, a robot? Your creator forget to program you with different seating options or something?"

I sighed. "Never mind."

I wasn't going to stay and listen to them laugh at me. I decided to just pick another seat. I found one at the back of the class, right next to a noisy fan that blew cool air in my face. It was not a good seat, but it was the only one left. That's what I get for wasting time arguing with the popular kids.

Mr. Turner entered the classroom.

"All right, class," he said. "Today is a pop quiz, so I hope you've all been paying attention during this unit."

Everyone groaned.

Mr. Turner handed out the quiz, and we all got to work.

I looked at my quiz. It didn't seem too difficult, just seven pages of trigonometry; I could practically do that in my sleep. The problem was I was too distracted. I always sit at the same desk, my spot. It's the perfect seat. It's too far from a fan or window to have an annoying draft, it's in a perfect position to properly see the blackboard, and it's close to the door, so when class is over, I have a head start at avoiding confrontation in the halls. The desk I was at now was the complete opposite, right at the back of the class and right next to a buzzing fan. Why was it even buzzing? Was it broken? What if it blows up? No, it's not going to blow up. It's probably just old, jammed up with dust or something. It'd be great if there were AC instead of this rattling fan. I don't understand why there's AC in the office but not in the classrooms. Well, I do. Money, obviously. But I still think it's a little unfair that the staff is being prioritized over the students. It gets really hot in a classroom full of teenagers.

Before I knew it, Mr. Turner said, "All right, pencils down. Class is over. Don't forget to hand in your quiz on the way out."

"What?" I blurted. "But I'm not finished."

The whole class laughed at my outburst.

"Perhaps next time you'll pay attention during my classes, Mr. McCoy," said Mr. Turner.

With my head down, I muttered to myself, "I was."

***

Later, on the bus ride home, I was doodling in my notebook, trying to keep out of trouble. In a lot of ways, the bus was like a mobile hallway. Someone's lunchbox was being thrown around, the person behind me wouldn't stop kicking my seat, it sounded like the people in front of me were making out, and I could hear someone saying something about tapping someone else's mother, whatever that means.

The only good thing about the bus was that it was slightly easier to be inconspicuous. If I kept my head down and didn't say anything, I could just be left to my own devices ... usually, but today was different.

Something hit me in the head—a crumpled-up piece of paper. I looked around and noticed the guy from my math class, Xavier, pointing at the paper. That can't be good. I unravelled it. It said, "Don't talk to my girl again." The message was accompanied by a crude drawing of what I assumed was supposed to be me with a face that made me look like a dim-witted cartoon character. He smirked at me.

I sighed and went back to doodling in my notebook. If I was certain of one thing in life, it was this: I hate school.

Chapter 2

Entering my two-storey, suburban house after the bus ride home, I cleaned my shoes on the floor mat and went into the kitchen.

"Hi, sweetie." My mom was washing up dishes, her long hair tied up in a bun so she wouldn't accidentally get it wet. "How was school?"

I grunted; she knew what it meant.

"That bad, huh?" my dad commented, coming in from the living room to sit at the circular table and do a crossword puzzle. He adjusted his glasses before starting on it.

"I had a math quiz," I explained.

"Oh, how'd you do?" He pencilled in an answer to his puzzle.

"Ran out of time. I got distracted like I always do, and I'm probably going to fail the class."

"Did you ask for an accommodation?" my mom asked.

"No."

"Charles, you know you need to ask for help when you're finding school difficult."

"Aren't they just supposed to give me the accommodation anyway? Why do I have to ask? Isn't the whole reason I got diagnosed to not have to ask?"

"The reason you got diagnosed was to have access to the help you need," said my dad. "There're a lot of kids in that school. You can't expect them to keep track of who needs what. You need to speak up for yourself."

"I can't do that. Everyone laughs at me as it is; getting special treatment will just add fuel to the fire."

"I do wish they would do a better job at accommodating the students who need help, though," my mom commented.

"That's life, I'm afraid," said my dad. "Everyone's got to be their own advocate." He looked at my face and added, "Don't worry about it, Charles. You're a smart kid. You may just find that you didn't do as badly as you think on that quiz."

Frustrated, I headed upstairs to my room without conjuring a response. Before I was completely out of earshot, though, my mom said, "Dinner's at six, Charles."

I grunted; she knew what it meant.

Opening my bedroom door, I breathed in the air of my sanctuary. Everything was exactly how I wanted it: bed on the left, desktop computer on the right (accompanied by a desk, of course), and a calendar with important dates hanging on the wall next to the window. This was my favourite place to be. I had complete control.

I closed my door and chucked my school bag on the floor. Then I pulled my phone out of my pocket and walked over to my calendar to update it. I know I have a calendar on my phone, but I like to be able to see what I've got coming up on the wall. It feels more concrete that way, helps me remember.

When I unlocked my phone, I saw that girl's number. Angela. I didn't have anything pencilled in for Friday. Should I go to the movies with her? That's not something I would usually do. I wouldn't know what to say or how to act. I know I said I would go but ... I took a pencil from atop the desk and wrote a "maybe" in the Friday slot.

Sighing, I booted up my computer. I'd think about that later; I had to de-stress, do something fun, like starting my IT assignment. I don't hate schoolwork; I love it. It's just school itself that I hate.

There was a knock at the door.

"Yeah?" I answered.

"It's me. Can I come in?" It sounded like my sister Ruby.

"Sure."

She entered. I didn't bother looking at her; it's not like I'd never seen her before. She's practically my female twin. Which is weird because she's seventeen, a whole three years older than me. Either I look old, or she looks young.

"What are you doing, bro?" she asked.

"IT assignment."

"Cool. Cool. Mind if I use your window?"

"What for?"

"To go see my girlfriend."

"I thought you were grounded."

"That's why I need your window. If my window's open then Mom and Dad will suspect something, but they won't care if your window's open."

"Makes sense."

"So can I use it?"

"If you promise not to involve me when you get into trouble, sure."

"Cool. Thanks, bro."

She walked to the window, but she didn't open it. "What's this?"

I looked to see what she was referring to. She was pointing at the "maybe" on my calendar.

"It's nothing," I said. "Some girl asked me to go to the movies with her."

"Shut the front door."

"It is shut."

"It's an expression. Who was this girl?"

"Her name's Angela."

"Is she cute?"

"I don't know. I didn't really notice."

"You didn't notice?" She leaned her hand on the desk. "Sometimes I can't believe you're my brother. Girls are hot, bro. Take the time to appreciate that every now and then."

"It doesn't matter. I'm probably not going anyway."

"What? Why not?"

"It's the movies."

"And?"

"It's too loud."

"Wear your earplugs."

"It's too crowded."

"Okay, bro, listen to me. I mean this with all the love I can possibly muster, you're being too autistic."

I looked at her. "How am I being too autistic? I am autistic. That's like saying you're being too allistic."

"Right. And when I am being too allistic, I let my little brother set me straight. You've got to listen to me, bro, go to the movies with her."

"I don't know," I sighed.

"How did this even happen? You have, like, no friends. How did you get invited to the movies?"

"I don't know. Some guys knocked my books on the ground, and she helped me pick them up. Then she started talking about seeing a movie together, and she gave me her number so I could let her know."

Ruby covered her mouth. She was either hiding a huge grin or holding back vomit. "Oh, my god, she likes you."

"Isn't that kind of obvious?"

"No, I mean she *really* likes you."

I stared at her, confused.

She chuckled. "You're going to make me spell it out, aren't you? She's romantically interested in you, Charles."

I paused. "Are you sure?"

"Ninety-eight percent sure."

"You realize that's a two percent error margin, right?"

"Better than three percent."

"Sure, I guess." I turned back to my computer screen. "She put her name into my phone as 'Ange' with a heart emoji next to it. What does that mean?"

"It means she's adorable. Perfect. You need to go out with her, get to know her."

"Why is her being adorable perfect?"

"Because it means she's probably kind and sensitive and patient, and even if you two don't hit it off romantically, she could be a good friend for you. You don't have many of those."

"I don't have *any* of those," I corrected.

"Exactly. Time to act allistic, bro. You got this."

"I guess it could be nice to know someone at school who doesn't hate me."

"That's the spirit." She walked over to the window and opened it. "Your window looks a bit more … precarious than mine. I guess this is where all my gymnastics lessons will pay off."

"Maxine must be quite a good girlfriend if you're willing to jump out of a window just to see her."

"Hey, Max is an excellent kisser; that's all the motivation I need."

"I'll take your word for it."

"Don't forget to text that girl."

"I won't."

"And you might want to close the window when I leave; it's kind of chilly. Laters." She dropped out the window, and I went to check that she got down safely. She slid down the drainpipe on the side of the house and made it to the ground unharmed. She gave me a thumbs-up, and I gave her the same.

Closing the window, I got my phone and stared at the screen, at the heart emoji next to Angela's name. With a progressively shaky hand, I started typing.

Chapter 3

The day was finally here—Friday. School was finished, I'd sorted everything out with Angela, and I had my parent's permission to go to the movies with her. All that was left to do was head to the movie theatre and meet up with Angela. It was close by, so I could walk there. Maybe the walk would help to calm my nerves. My heart was racing, and I was having trouble breathing. That always happened whenever I would do something too social for my taste. But Ruby's right. This could be good for me. Even if our dad catching her sneaking back into the house late last night somewhat undermined her point.

Either way, I just had to keep focused on the one thing: (*wear me*) walking to the movie theatre … Wait, what was that? (*Wear me.*) There it is again. Am I thinking that? (*Wear me.*) I can't be; those aren't my thoughts.

In the distance was a glimmer of light etched into the sidewalk. It was just a few metres away, and I couldn't shake the feeling that it was calling to me. (*Wear me.*)

I walked toward it, and as I came closer, it took a more recognizable shape—a ring. I picked it up. (*Wear me.*) It was just a shiny golden ring with some engraved writing that I couldn't decipher. It definitely wasn't English (*wear me*) or any recognizable language for that matter. As I brought it closer to my finger (*wear me*), I realized how much I wanted ... to wear it.

I put it on.

It was silent—no cars, no wind, nothing. The foreign thoughts had gone. I could just barely hear my own breath. And then the silence was broken. There was a crumbling sound, like falling rocks, coming from behind. When I turned to look, I realized that the ground itself was crumbling away, engulfed by an abyss of darkness. I ran in the other direction, but it wasn't just the ground that was crumbling, it was the houses, the streetlights, even the birds soaring high in the sky were still being sucked down, piece by piece, into the abyss below. I couldn't outrun it; the ground in front of me was crumbling, too. The world was literally falling apart, and eventually, I succumbed and crumbled as well.

Now there was nothing but complete darkness. Though I had crumbled to pieces a few seconds ago, I felt fine now—I was whole again. A harsh light hit me, then another, and another after that. The lights weren't coming from bulbs; they were coming from eyeballs. Monolithic, floating eyeballs about three times my size, with eyelids enabling them to blink at me and flicker their lights on and off. I looked down, away from the lights, but the whole ground was one gargantuan eyeball shining a light that felt like needles to my retinas. Its eyelids began to creep closed, and I was slowly sinking into its pupil. When the eyelids shut, I was trapped, and it was dark once again.

The eyelids opened, and the harsh light returned, but this time, I was underneath them. The light shone above my head and down to my feet, and from those feet emerged a shadow darker than I had words for. It contrasted with the light, attacked its brightness with its darkness. It grew from my feet like a puddle and then escaped the ground that trapped it. It stood before me, and with an added dash of colour, it looked just like me ... Or maybe I looked like it. It came closer, and no matter how much the light beamed down, it only contrasted against it, looking darker and darker. It was when we were eye to eye that its very flesh melted off its bones, and those bones buckled and broke, crumbling to the ground in a heap of ash.

The only thing left intact in that heap of ash was its skull, and from the eye sockets and jawbone, the eight-legged creatures scurried out. Pitch-black spiders, tons of them, crawling up my legs, consuming my body with nothing more than their large number. I could hear the crumple of their little legs; I could feel all eight of them on my skin. They crawled and spread, completely covering my face. There were so many that they blocked out the light, and the mass of arachnids weighed enough to topple me to the ground. They could have crushed me, killed me without an ounce of venom, but instead, they scurried away. Not out of kindness.

The light was bright again as it approached me. Every step it took was equal to an earthquake. If millions of tiny spiders were bad, then one gigantic spider could only be worse. It focused its eyes on me—all eight of them, blinking them at different rates, and I could hear the creaking squelch as each lid closed. It was a towering monster that I'd only ever seen in horror movies, and I was a fly, afraid for my life. I tried to stand, to run, but I was too heavy. The smaller spiders were gone, but I could still feel their weight keeping me grounded. That's what I thought, at least, but a glance at my arm showed me the truth. I was caught in a huge spider web. I could pull all I wanted, but my skin would rip off before I would ever get free. The webbing pulled on my neck, forcing me to look into the spider's eight, red eyes. But then those eight became two. Its eight legs became four. The spider's entire body was anthropomorphizing to such an extent that it was no longer a spider, just a black shadow with glowing, red eyes.

It launched a hand toward me, wrapping its fingers around my body like tentacles. They felt wet and rubbery. It lifted me up, and the webbing dragged me down, stretching my skin. It lifted me higher and higher, but no matter how much my skin stretched, it wouldn't snap, it wouldn't break, it only burned. A smile grew upon the shadow's face, and sharp teeth protruded from that smile. Slowly, as the shadow's hand lifted me above its head, and its mouth stretched to the size of a football field, the web finally snapped, and I was dropped in and swallowed.

Then there was light, and birds, and a ground beneath my feet. I was back where I'd started when I put the ring on. But not everything was back to normal.

A scream was the only sound I could hear. It started as a high-pitched screech but gradually lowered into a thunderous roar. And as the pitch lowered, so did I. I fell to the ground again—paralyzed.

The last thing I saw was the golden ring locked around my finger. It flashed red three times, and then there was darkness again.

Chapter 4

"**W**elcome, one and all, to the Planet of Shadows."

A voice spoke, deep, demonic, and unfamiliar. It sent a shiver down my spine, but it was the only sign I had to prove I was still alive. It was completely dark. I couldn't see myself, I couldn't hear myself, I couldn't even feel myself. For all I knew, that ring had killed me ... That ring. What was it? I should be dead. But I'm not; I don't believe it. I don't believe in life after death. If you're dead, you're dead; there's no way around it. You just don't exist anymore. So the fact that I can hear a voice telling me about this "Planet of Shadows" means that I'm not dead ... yet.

The voice continued. "You all must have many questions. Allow me to answer them for you. My leader has instructed me to gather data for an experiment. To accomplish this, I have collected two creatures from each of the fifty eligible planets throughout this galaxy. This totals one hundred specimens with which to gather the required data.

"Here's how this will work: The Planet of Shadows is where you shall all reside for an indefinite amount of time. I constructed this planet myself using elements of the fifty planets whence you all came. As such, you shall all have advantages and disadvantages whilst you are here. It took ten years to construct the Planet of Shadows, so do not be alarmed if you notice any changes to your physical forms.

"For those of you who are having difficulty comprehending what I am saying, you may imagine that this is a game in which the goal is to survive. Every one of you will soon be placed on the planet's surface, and none shall return to their home unless they are the last surviving creature. This is a test of adaptability, as the planet shall not remain the same. It will change constantly, and new opportunities shall arise just as often as old ones fade away.

"Some of you may be desperate to return to your homes and might be driven to murder the others here in order to ensure that you are the last one standing. Though I will not prohibit such an action, I will deter it. Be warned, the mark of a killer is everlasting. Every creature will be able to identify the soul of a murderer by a killer's blood-red eyes.

"And with that, I wish you all luck, and welcome again to the Planet of Shadows."

***

My eyes shot open. I lay flat on my back in the middle of a sprawling forest. Light struggled to break through the thick tree barrier. It was humid and moist, and I was detecting the incongruous scent of chlorine.

I brought my trembling hand to my face. The ring was gone.

I slowly came to my feet, and naturally, the heat and humidity felt worse. But I could feel. I could smell. I could see. I was alive.

I thought for a second. The voice I'd heard spoke about a "Planet of Shadows." Is that where I was? Maybe this was a dream. Maybe I was so nervous about going to the movies with Angela that I conjured up this stress-fueled nightmare. That makes sense, much more sense than putting on a psychosis-inducing ring and being taken to an alien planet with the goal of being the last survivor. This was definitely a dream ... But I can't dream something I've never seen before, can I? Dreams are an amalgamation of lived experiences. You can't dream about something you've never experienced, and the trees in this forest are the weirdest trees I've ever seen. I didn't know a word that could accurately describe the colour of the bark, but the trees looked like rubbery, tightly coiled springs. I couldn't have dreamed it; I barely even knew how to properly describe it.

I don't think I'm dreaming.

Wait a minute. Didn't that voice say something about the planet's construction taking ten years? I looked at my hand again. The ring was still gone, but my hand looked bigger. There was hair on my arms that wasn't there before. Could it really have been ten years since I found the ring? That would make me twenty-four years old now.

"No, I'm not twenty-four. That's crazy," I said, and then I immediately covered my mouth.

My voice ... it was deeper, fuller.

Oh, my god.

I was hyperventilating now. How did this happen? How did walking to the movie theatre to watch a movie with a girl I met in school result in this? I wiped my forehead and sweat came off of it. It was hot, humid. I couldn't breathe, couldn't think right. I had to get out of this forest. I had to find someplace cooler.

I took a step and unleashed a cracking sound—a twig breaking underneath my feet. This was immediately followed by a swarm of some kind. I hit the ground face first as a reflex action. I had no idea what was going on, but it felt like an earthquake, and it sounded like a whirlwind. I looked up slightly while still keeping my head down. The word *swarm* wasn't too far off. There were hundreds of flying insects, zipping all over the place. They looked a lot like butterflies. Their wings sparkled, reflecting what little light could penetrate the tree leaves. There was one difference between these things and butterflies, though: where a butterfly would have smoothly rounded wings, these creatures had jagged wings, as if they were made of many overlapping triangles.

The swarm eventually died down. Each of the insects found a branch to perch itself upon. They stared absently with beady red eyes that looked and sounded like a camera shutter every time they blinked.

I waited for my heart to slow down, though I had trouble believing it ever would. The insects must have reacted to the twig I'd stepped on. I had to be more careful. If all of this truly is real, then everything I'm seeing here—the trees, the insects—it's all alien, as in extraterrestrial. Probably best not to provoke things you know nothing about.

I slowly stood again and then immediately ducked back down as the swarm feverishly resumed. The sound was so loud, like being in a windstorm. Maybe it wasn't the twig they were reacting to; maybe it was my movements. If that's the case, how am I supposed to get out of this forest? Maybe ... maybe I should just try to walk through the swarm. I mean, they're just insects, right? They don't appear to have stingers or anything. Maybe I can just walk through them and be fine. I crept my gaze upward. They fluttered around so quickly and violently. And their wings had a lot of jagged edges; they looked sharp. Maybe it's not the best idea to just assume that they wouldn't hurt me. I don't even know what they are. They could have poisonous skin, or laser eyes, or I don't know what else … But they hadn't hurt me yet; they hadn't even touched me. In fact, it looked like they didn't want to fly too low to the ground. Maybe they couldn't … Well, I guess that's a better idea than walking through and hoping they won't hurt me. I took a deep breath and started crawling.

It was working. They were still zipping around, probably because I was still moving, but they weren't harming me. The ground still shook like an earthquake, though, and it still felt like I was in the middle of a tornado. But I'm alive.

After a few minutes, I saw a light coming from an opening between the trees. Maybe it was an exit. I picked up my pace and crawled through the opening.

I was right; I was out of the forest. The swarm was gone, and it was instantly quieter. There was just ambient noise now, like chirping birds. But there were also sounds I couldn't place—ticking, crumpling, and a whistle that repeated at the speed of a marching band's snare drum.

I stood up very slowly. No swarm came after me. I was safe. I couldn't smell chlorine anymore, and it wasn't as humid, but it was still hot. I was in some sort of derelict desert with bright yellow sand stretching all the way to the horizon. The topography was pretty flat—not too many plants or rocks around. The forest was the tallest thing here. The sky was hazy and purple, but it didn't seem like nighttime. It was bright enough to see, and there were no stars in the sky.

In the distance, I thought I could see a person walking by. Maybe they knew where I was, what had happened to me. As I approached, I realized that the person wasn't exactly human. They looked like a human—a man, but the complexion of his skin was a glistening cerulean, his ears were droopy and rectangular, and he had white, stringy hair. I went back and forth on whether I should talk to him, but eventually, I was close enough for him to stare at me, probably wondering who I was and why I had approached him.

"Um, hello," I said. He looked a little more human now that I could see his face.

"Hi." He smiled. He sounded human, too.

"Uh ..." I scratched the back of my head. "I ... I don't mean to, um ... can you ... can you tell me where I am?"

"The Planet of Shadows, apparently, at least according to that voice."

"You mean ... you heard it, too?"

"I think everyone did, yeah."

"Everyone?"

"As the voice said, there are one hundred people here, taken from fifty different planets."

I paused to let this all sink in.

"You okay?" he asked me.

"I don't know," I admitted.

He rubbed his chin. "I'm not familiar with your kind. Tell me, how advanced is your species in the field of space travel?"

"Uh, I don't know. We've sent a bunch of probes out into space, to take pictures and stuff."

"I meant manned travel. Have you ever been to another planet?"

"Well, *I* haven't, but there are people who have gone to the moon."

He nodded. "Okay, and where is 'the moon' in relation to your home planet?"

"Right next to it; it orbits the planet."

"I see. Not very advanced at all. This must be terrifying for you. Did you come from that forest?" He pointed to the mass of trees behind me.

"Yeah."

"That's twitchfly territory; how did you escape?"

"What's a twitchfly?"

He squinted his eyes at me. "You know, large insects with very angular wings. They usually fly in massive swarms."

"They're called twitchflies?"

"Yeah, they're native to the planet Kcyyck. Very dangerous creatures. I'm surprised someone who's never even heard of them managed to get away."

"Yeah, I just realized that they didn't like to fly too low to the ground, and I crawled out ... Sorry, where did you say they were from?"

"Kcyyck. Like *kah-seek*, but it's only one syllable. Kcyyck. It's a tiny, little green planet. I could probably point it out for you if the stars were visible in the sky. Maybe another time."

I was silent.

"You're very lucky, though," he continued. "Twitchflies are known to decapitate anyone who gets caught up in their swarm."

"Decapitate?" I blurted.

"Yes, it's quite brutal. But you managed to escape without ever having heard of a twitchfly. You must have good survival instincts. Smart, intuitive, adaptable."

"I don't know about that last one."

He smiled. "Perhaps we can help each other out. What are you called?"

"What am I called?"

"Yes. What are you called by your species?"

"You mean my name?"

"If that's what you call it."

"Um, Charles."

"Good to meet you, Charles. I am called Skylar." He reached out his hand for a handshake, but I just stared at it blankly. "I'm sorry, does shaking hands mean something vulgar on your planet?"

"Uh, no, no it doesn't. I just don't like handshakes."

"Fair enough." He pulled his hand back. "Come with me. There are some people I'd like you to meet."

Chapter 5

After a short walk through the desert, Skylar and I arrived at an old cabin. It didn't look very inviting. There was mould growing from between the wooden walls, and it looked damp and splintery. Though, frankly, I wasn't as shocked by the condition of the cabin as I was by the fact that there was a cabin here in the first place. I was just beginning to wrap my head around being on an alien planet and being ten years older. I hadn't even imagined that there could be housing here, too. Though, I suppose the whole planet couldn't just be deserts and forests. Maybe there could even be a city around somewhere.

"Is this your cabin?" I asked Skylar.

"Yes and no. I found it abandoned on my travels. I've just been crashing here." He walked toward the cabin door. "Come on."

I followed him in.

There was only one room inside, but it served the purpose of three. There were a couple of small beds in the far corner, a little kitchen off to the side, and in the centre, a large living room of sorts, though it didn't have any furniture.

In the living room area were two people sitting on the floor. One looked about four feet tall and had a single eye in the centre of his face and a single antenna on the crown of his head. The other one looked to be my height, but she had a hairless tail and thin tentacles coming out of her head. They almost resembled hair.

"Trish, Waxton, this is Charles." Skylar introduced me to the others. "Charles, this is Trish," he pointed to the tentacle-haired one, "and this is Waxton," he pointed to the one-eyed one.

"Uh ... hi," I said.

"Thou bring more?" said Waxton, ignoring me and directing his attention to Skylar. "We talk 'bout this."

"We can't have a resistance with only three people," Skylar explained.

"Can, if try. More, bad. Not know enough. Easy danger."

"I'm sorry," I interrupted. "This is a resistance?"

They all looked at me.

"Yes, it is," Skylar answered, smiling.

"What are you resisting?"

"The one who brought us to this planet."

"You mean the voice?"

"I do. That voice said we are all here to help gather data for an experiment. It said two people were selected from each of fifty eligible planets."

I nodded. "Okay, yeah. That voice is experimenting on us. I can see why you'd want to resist."

"Not only that, I think that voice wasn't being entirely truthful. Think about it. It said fifty *eligible* planets. Eligible for what? What makes a planet eligible? I've been noticing some strange things here. Firstly, everyone partaking in the experiment that I've encountered so far is humanoid. The planet adjacent to mine is dominated by nehks, but they have a feline form. Were they not eligible to be here because of that? Also, it seems that there is a fairly equal number of males and females here. I've encountered no other variation in sex. Does that mean the two people selected from each planet were one male and one female? Why? Sexual diversity? Reproductive purposes?"

"Only, not that," Waxton cut in. "All speak same tongue."

"Yes," Skylar continued. "Though, our grammatical practices are still different, suggesting that we're all actually speaking different languages, and our speech is being universally translated somehow."

"I guess that's possible," I agreed. "But what's your point? The voice said this was a test of our adaptability to collect data for an experiment. What makes you think that's not the truth?"

"I believe that's the truth but not the whole truth. If it's just our adaptability being tested, why are the test subjects exclusively humanoid? Why is it essential that we all are able to communicate with each other? And this person who's conducting the experiment, how did they create this planet in the first place? I've never seen anyone who could pull that off. I just get the feeling that the data being collected for this experiment is being used for a very specific purpose. And I'm not so certain I believe that purpose is an innocent one."

Skylar was interrupted by a faint laughter that gradually got louder. It was coming from Trish, who had elected to remain silent until now. "I think that you are taking all of this too seriously," she said. "The voice said that this is a game. That is how we should think of it."

"I think that was just a comparison," I said. "This isn't an actual game."

"If you think that this is real, then you are a fool. No one can create a planet like this. No one can invade fifty planets in secret and abduct two people from each of them. It is madness. This is just a game."

Now that Trish was speaking, I had more incentive to look in her direction. I'm not usually one to look people in the eye, but all it took was a small glance for me to realize that Trish's eyes were red—the blood-red eyes of a killer. The voice's words echoed in my mind.

I stepped back a bit. "You're a murderer."

"I am not!" she shouted. "I am a saviour. I help people escape this game in the fastest possible way: losing."

"But losing means dying. You're killing people."

"I am not killing anyone. They are not dying. These are all lies."

"How do you know that?"

"I have already told you: This is a game." She crossed her arms. "We are all in a simulation, and when we die, we will be back home. People scribe stories about this sort of thing on my planet. They tell the tales of contestants brought to a virtual world to compete in a game of survival. That is what this is."

That made sense. I've read those kinds of stories, too. But her reasoning was still off. "If that's what you believe, why are you part of a resistance?"

"It is safer in a group. This is a very dangerous place."

"But you said this was just a game. What do you care if you die?"

"I do not want to die painfully. I save others by killing them quickly. They will not feel a thing, and they will return home safely." She paused for a bit. "I would also like to know who abducted us. I have been here for a week already, and I miss my child."

"A week?" I blurted. "I only just woke up. I can't have been unconscious here for a week."

"We all woke up at different times," Skylar explained. "Waxton here has been on the planet for a month. The running theory is that it takes different amounts of time for each of us to become accustomed to the conditions of this planet, and only after we have do we wake up. This is a foreign planet for all of us—different air, different gravity. Yet we're all accustomed to it like we've been here for years."

"Have," commented Waxton. "We here ten years."

"The ten-year thing happened to you, too?" I said. "Did you find a golden ring before you got here?"

They all shook their heads.

"I had a questionable meal," said Trish.

"Me, find odd bug," said Waxton.

"I just had a strange dream," said Skylar.

My heart was pounding again. This was real. This was all real. It wasn't just me. There were other people here—aliens. This was happening to them, too.

"So, Charles." Skylar brushed back his stringy, white hair. "If you're interested, we'd love to have you join us."

"Join you?" I questioned.

"Yeah. Just to be clear, we don't kill people. That's Trish's opinion; she doesn't speak for the group." Trish rolled her red eyes. "We're interested in finding out who brought us here and what they want with us. We could use someone like you, someone who's smart and able to think on their toes."

I thought about it. Being in a group might not be so bad. We could all watch each other's backs. I'd be safer. But Trish's red eyes reminded me that I might not be safe at all. She hasn't killed Skylar and Waxton, though. But she could still try to kill me.

"I don't know," I admitted.

"How about you shadow us tomorrow," Skylar suggested. "You can get a feel for the resistance. Then you can make your decision afterward. No pressure. If you want to walk away, you can walk away. I just thought we could all help each other out."

Admittedly, it didn't sound so bad, but I hardly knew these people. I didn't think this was a decision I could make analytically. I had to use my gut. I have to act allistic, like Ruby always says.

"Um, okay," I said. "I'll stay and decide tomorrow."

Skylar smiled, but I couldn't tell if that meant something good or something bad.

"I no like," Waxton said. "This, bad idea."

Skylar looked at me, then at Trish, and then at Waxton. "We'll see. I've got a good feeling about this."

Chapter 6

Trish, Skylar, Waxton, and I were all spending the day picking berries in a forest—a different one from the one I woke up in ... I think. There were no twitchflies here, at least.

I plucked a yellow berry from a tree and placed it among the other yellow berries in my wooden basket. I was a little amazed that there were wooden baskets on this planet. Skylar said he found them in the cabin when he first got there. I wonder who made them.

"It's okay to mix them, you know," said Skylar as he picked a berry next to me.

"What do you mean?" I wondered.

"There are only yellow berries in your basket. We'll be here forever if you only pick one colour of berry at a time. Just throw them all in. But not the purple ones; I think those are poisonous."

"No, blue poison," Waxton butt in. "Purple taste bad."

"That's right. I remember now," said Skylar. "Thanks, Waxton."

Waxton waved and then climbed up a tree to reach a large bunch of berries. Due to his height, he couldn't reach them by standing alone.

"Anyway," I continued, "I didn't mean to only pick the yellow berries. Yellow is my favourite colour, and I like things to match. I must have subconsciously picked just the yellow ones."

"No harm done." Skylar shrugged.

"Why are we collecting berries anyway? I thought you said there was food in the cabin."

"Food for us, yeah. But ten years have passed since the time we were all abducted."

"So?"

"Because of that, some of us are in our prime, and others are now old and feeble."

"So we're collecting berries to help feed the people who are too old to find food for themselves?"

"That's correct." He nodded.

I'd never considered that the ten-year time gap could be to some people's detriment. It made me twenty-four years old, so I felt just fine. But for other people, who may have been old to begin with, the time-lapse wouldn't have been a very good thing at all.

Suddenly, a scream made me cover my ears as it shattered the tranquillity around us. Skylar and I looked at each other and then ran in the direction of the sound. When we arrived, just a few trees away, we found Trish trembling on the ground and pointing at a tree in front of her.

"Trish, what's wrong?" Skylar asked.

"It is up there. It is disgusting."

I curiously walked to where she was pointing. On one of the tree's branches, there was a small, furry, worm-like creature.

"I've seen this before," I said. "It's a caterpillar."

"I do not care what it is. Get it away from me," Trish demanded.

"It's not that bad, Trish," Skylar laughed, helping her up to her feet.

"It is ugly, and squirmy, and creepy. Why can it not look like that one?" She pointed at another creature—a small, flying insect.

"That's a butterfly," I exclaimed. I never thought I'd be so happy to see one.

"That one has pretty wings," said Trish. "Why can that worm not have pretty wings?"

"Believe it or not, that butterfly was once like this caterpillar."

"You are joking."

"No, really. A caterpillar eats leaves and other food, and then one day, it moults its skin and reveals this shiny cocoon called a chrysalis. After that, it emerges from that chrysalis as a butterfly."

"In that case, I do not like the flying one either." She crossed her arms.

"Calm, Trish," said Waxton, finally arriving at where we all were. It must have taken him a bit of time to climb down that tree. "Bugs small. Nothing to fear."

"Easy for you to say," Trish mumbled.

"I take it these caterpillars and butterflies are native to your planet, Charles?" Skylar asked.

"Yeah, they're all over the place in the summertime. I don't even like them much, but it's amazing how you can love something familiar when you're surrounded by the unfamiliar."

"I know what you mean," said Trish. "On my planet, there are these ugly, dangerous things called Tarjix. They are hairy and have eleven eyeballs but only two eyelids. They vomit out their insides and spray you with acid. I used to dread seeing them, but now, I would kill to see one."

There was a pause—a small moment in which everyone took the time to appreciate what we had lost. The moment ended when Skylar insisted, "We should start bringing all these berries back now. I imagine everyone is starving."

***

Later on, we all arrived at some sort of ruins. It looked like it was possibly the centre of a town with a fountain in the middle, but now everything was covered in sand and rocks, and the supposed fountain in the centre only slightly resembled what I thought it to be.

The ruins were populated by many different people—all with different skin tones, body features, and home planets. One person—an old man—approached me. He looked quite human actually, aside from the eight tentacles he used for legs. I handed him some of the berries we'd picked earlier, as Skylar had instructed me to do. The man thanked me and slithered away on his tentacle legs.

"You know," Skylar said, walking up to me, "at the end of the day, I think this is what makes everything worth it."

"What do you mean?" I asked.

"This job, this little resistance, it's not easy. We're always travelling and tending to people's needs, and we don't even know if we can find the one who abducted us or if we can get everyone safely off this planet. I mean, before all this happened, I was just starting out as an intergalactic police officer."

"There are intergalactic police officers?" I interrupted.

He pulled on his droopy rectangular ears and smiled at me. "You come from a pretty infantile planet when it comes to space travel. The police don't bother planets like that, just ones who are into interplanetary trade and diplomacy. But I wasn't expecting to go from that to this, you know? I was fresh out of the academy, and now I'm here, doing what I can to help. That's the point of this resistance, in the end, to help people. It's nice to see that come to fruition, even if it's just feeding the elderly for the moment."

I nodded. Trish, Skylar, Waxton, all of them seemed like good people. Selfless. Definitely nothing like the people I used to interact with in school. Maybe it wouldn't be a bad idea to join their group. It's funny. Back on Earth, I never really connected with others; I didn't socialize very often. It was exhausting, and I felt like an alien most of the time. But here, everyone is an alien, and so no one is. Who knew, far away from Earth, far away from human beings, I would feel so at home?

Suddenly, the air vibrated with a strange sound. Like a power drill screwing a nail into a wall.

"Do you hear that?" asked Skylar.

"Yeah, what is it?"

"Trouble. Big trouble." Skylar waved his hands and got everyone's attention. "Everyone, listen up, we need to evacuate these ruins, right now."

"What wrong?" Waxton asked, coming over to us.

"There's something out here that doesn't want us in these ruins," Skylar said. He was looking around in every direction. "Waxton, get Trish and help to evacuate everyone before it's too late. I just hope that sound isn't what I think it is."

Waxton nodded and started rounding everyone up so that he and Trish could escort them out of the area.

The ground began to shake, and my heart beat rapidly. Then the ground in front of us was swallowed up by a huge hole, and from it, a brown, furry, four-legged creature emerged. It was the size of a grizzly bear, and it had a long fluffy tail with a spinning metal drill at the tip. Its ears and nose were rather small, but its eyes were large and fully black, and its mouth was huge and gaping, drool dripping from the corners. Every tooth it had was a spinning drill, the force of which made the creature's whole body tremor.

"Charles, run," Skylar said quietly, without really looking at me.

I was frozen, scared out of my mind.

"Charles?"

The creature raised its tail. It was about to attack.

"Charles, look out!" Skylar pushed me to safety, and the creature's tail penetrated the ground where I once stood, drilling it into dust.

Skylar took me behind a large rock, out of the creature's sight.

I tried to slow my breathing. "What is that thing?"

"A drillmite."

"A drill *mite*? I thought mites were supposed to be small, like dust mites."

"Maybe on your planet, but this is an average-sized drillmite. Nasty-looking one, too." Skylar peeked at it from behind the rock. "Okay, here's what we're going to do: Drillmites are territorial; this one won't leave us alone until we're dead. We're going to have to distract it, and if we're lucky, it will forget that we were ever here. They're not the smartest of creatures."

I was silent.

"Charles, are you with me?"

"Huh? Yeah, yeah, I'm just ..."

He looked at me. "I know you must be scared. I promise I won't let anything happen to you, but you have to do as I say."

I took a deep breath. "Yeah, okay, how are we meant to distract it?"

Skylar paused for a moment, looking at the basket of berries I was clutching onto. Miraculously, there were still berries in it, despite many falling out during the commotion. Skylar didn't even have his basket anymore; he dropped it when he pushed me out of the way. "We'll use the berries," he said finally. "We'll throw them at the drillmite's eyes and blind it. It'll stop to clean the berries out of its eyes, and then we'll escape. By the time it's done and sees that we aren't there, it'll forget about us and go about its business."

Before another word was spoken, the rock we were using for cover was pulverized by the drillmite's crushing maw. Skylar and I both ran, but in the confusion, we got separated. The drillmite went after Skylar, who responded by picking up some berries off the ground and chucking them at the creature's big black eyes. It let out a cry, almost like the sound a cat makes when their tail has been stepped on.

Then, like the crack of a whip, the drillmite turned its attention to me. Berry juice was covering its eyes but not completely. Its eyes were huge; there was a lot of space to cover. It approached, and I froze. Its tail rose, and the drill spun so violently that it rattled like the tail of a rattlesnake. I saw some berries on the ground next to me, but I couldn't pick them up. I couldn't move. I couldn't do anything.

"Hey!" Skylar threw another berry at it. "You're not done with me yet."

This time, the drillmite unleashed a sound that was like the roar of a panther. It turned and charged at Skylar.

I still couldn't move. I just stared as Skylar struggled to keep his distance and pelted the creature with more berries. The drillmite loped after him like a cat hunting a mouse, and the ground rumbled every time its tail slid over it.

Someone grabbed my hand, and I clenched up. I hate when people touch me; it makes me feel violated. I turned to see who it was: Waxton.

"We go!" he said.

He dragged me over to where he and Trish had taken all the elderly—the bottom of a little sand dune. Trish made a gesture, flapping her hands inward. When we made it to her, she yelled, "Skylar, come on!"

Skylar threw one last berry, and it landed dead in the centre of one of the drillmite's eyes. The drillmite finally stopped. It plunged its head into the ground like an ostrich does. Maybe it was using the sand to clean its face. Skylar took the opportunity to get away and regroup with us.

"Is everyone all right?" he asked when he got to us.

There were a lot of yeses and nods and other things of that nature, but there was no response from me. Frankly, I didn't know if I was "all right." I'd never been more afraid in my whole life.

"Are you all right, Skylar?" asked Trish.

Skylar was rubbing his cheek. "I think so. A piece of rock caught me on the jaw. I'll be fine."

"We past ruins border," Waxton said. "We safe."

"Not yet," Skylar responded. "We have to make sure the drillmite's forgotten about us."

We all held our breath and watched as the drillmite pulled its head back out of the ground. It looked around the area for a bit and then unleashed its panther-like roar again. I got the sense it was angry, but it just jumped on top of a nearby rock and crushed it, playing with the fallen debris like a cat would play with a bug.

Skylar sighed. "Now we're safe."

***

At the end of the day, after we helped the elderly find suitable shelter for the night—caves, huts, and even more cabins—we all returned to Skylar's cabin.

"Well, that was quite the day." Trish stretched and yawned. "I think I will go to sleep now."

"Don't forget, Trish, it's your turn to do the dishes," said Skylar, though Trish was already on her way inside, and it didn't look like she heard him.

"I tell her," said Waxton as he followed Trish inside.

"Are you all right, Charles?" Skylar asked me. He was still rubbing his cheek. "You've been pretty quiet."

"Yeah, I'm fine, I guess."

"Good. I'm glad we all made it through today safely."

"Yeah," I said absently.

"Have you given any thought to my offer for you to stay with us?"

"I have."

"And?"

I looked at his cheek. It wasn't blue anymore; it was green. It looked like it was starting to swell. "Honestly, I ... I can't. I can't stay with you."

He looked down. "I see."

"I'm sorry." I couldn't really tell if he was upset, but that felt like the right thing to say.

"No, it's fine. Like I told you, there's no pressure to stay. I can't say I'm not surprised by your answer, though. I thought ... Do you mind my asking what led to your decision?"

"The drillmite. Seeing how everyone acted, how I acted. I just froze while everyone else sprung into action."

"You were scared. There's nothing wrong with that. Drillmites are terrifying creatures."

"But you weren't scared. Neither was Trish or Waxton."

"We all come from planets with advanced space travel. We see dangerous alien creatures all the time. I mean, you can't tell me your planet doesn't have creatures just as dangerous."

"Not ones I expect to see regularly." I took a breath. "I'm not like you, Skylar. I can't deal with that. You got hurt because I didn't do anything."

"That's not your fault."

"But it is. If I had just helped and thrown the berries like you said, we could have stopped the drillmite faster, and maybe you wouldn't have gotten hurt."

"Or maybe I would have," he countered.

"I don't want to find out. I don't want anyone getting hurt or killed because I'm not brave enough, or fast enough, or strong enough. I can't live with that. I'll only be a liability to you."

He stroked his droopy ears. "I don't see it that way. But I understand. If this is how you think it should be, then so be it. It was nice meeting you, Charles." He offered his hand for a handshake but retracted it quickly. "Sorry, I almost forgot. You don't like handshakes."

I smiled. "Tell Trish and Waxton I said *bye*."

"You don't want to stay with us for the night?"

"No, I need to go. I'm sorry."

"Okay, sure. Oh, wait. There's something I want to give you." Skylar rushed into the cabin, and then he came back out and handed me a small leather bag.

"A satchel?" I questioned.

He nodded.

I opened it.

"Berries for the road," he confirmed. "It's not much, they probably won't last you more than two meals, but it's something."

"Wow, this is great." I looked at the berries more closely and grinned. "They're all yellow."

"I thought you might like that. I salvaged what I could find while we were finding everyone shelter. Saved all the yellow ones for you."

"Wow, I don't know what to say. Thank you."

"It's the least I can do. Stay safe. You don't need me to tell you that this place is dangerous. And you always have a place with us, if you ever change your mind."

Skylar and I went our separate ways. I strapped the leather satchel over my shoulder for easy access. Even though I was on an alien planet and there wasn't another human being in sight, today, I felt that I'd truly made a friend.

Chapter 7

My travels brought me to a dense, snowy tundra, though it felt almost as warm as a desert. I was sweating, but whenever a snowflake touched my skin, it still felt cold. Around me stood tall ice structures that seemed to have been erected for living purposes—within them were ice chairs, ice tables, and other such ice-based furniture. There didn't seem to be anyone in them, though. The structures were abandoned.

While I walked, I finished the rest of the berries Skylar had given me. And then I was left with an empty satchel, meaning I would soon have to start thinking about how I would get more food. I used to think surviving the school halls was stressful. It seems trivial now that I have to think about food, water, and shelter. And then there're all the dangerous creatures here, most of which I've never even heard of.

A howling sound floated by in the wind. Curious, I followed it, although, in hindsight, that wasn't the best idea. Curiosity popped into my head for a split second, and I didn't think twice about acting on it. That's a trait of autism, a trait that might just get me killed if I'm not careful.

The sound led me to the ruins of what was probably another huge ice structure. Within, there was a small man, pinned to the ground by his injuries. I ran to his aid, but on the way, I caught sight of something out of the corner of my eye. I thought it was a bear, but when I turned to look, there was nothing. I was probably just jumpy; that drillmite still lived in the back of my mind.

I crouched down next to the man. He was tiny and old, and he had purple skin and a short, white beard.

"Are you all right?" I asked him, wiping sweat from my forehead.

"Me for late too it's," he whispered.

"What?"

"Great too are injuries my; on go can't I."

I paused, trying to decipher what he was saying. "Are you speaking backward?"

"You understand don't I." The man squinted at me.

"Um ... help need you do?" I spoke slowly, as I was struggling to correctly state my sentence backward.

"Dangerous is world this," he coughed. "You help to me for late too not it's but, me help to you for late too it's."

"Wait, uh ... sentences smaller in speak. This to new I'm."

The man reached into the snow and pulled out a bottle of sparkling water—not carbonated water, water that sparkled like a diamond. He looked at me. "I speak as you do now, so you do not mistake my words."

I was silent, flabbergasted that he could speak properly. Why was I struggling to speak backward this whole time? He was speaking a little slower now, though. Maybe this was just as hard for him as speaking backward was for me.

"Take this water." He handed me the bottle of sparkling water. "This planet is home to many dangerous creatures; it's not a place for one such as yourself. By drinking this water, your strength, speed, and durability will improve, and you will be able to protect yourself against the creatures here. However, you must be careful. The water inflicts madness upon those who drink it." He reached back into the snow and pulled out a worn, brown leather bracelet. "Hand your me give."

It took me a second to decipher the last part, but when I did, I put my hand out, and he wrapped the bracelet around my wrist.

"This will protect you from the madness," he said. "Don't ever drink the water without the bracelet on. Do you understand?"

I was silent.

"Tell me you understand. This water will save you. You will not survive without it."

I could see the drillmite in the back of my mind. I remembered how I just froze. "I understand," I said.

"Good. If you run out of the water, you'll need to find more. There are natural springs scattered all over the planet. You'll need to find the ones that contain sparkling water. It's important that you always have enough ... You for do can I all is that. Luck ... good." Then he was silent. He had succumbed to his injuries.

I looked at the clear, glistening water bottle in my hand. Would it really make me stronger? What if it was poison, and this was all just a trick? Well, I guess, in a way, it is poison. That's what the bracelet is for. I looked at the bracelet for a second, but then my eyes went back to the water. For a moment, I just sat there, deep in thought, as the water twinkled in the bottle. Then I stood up and went on my way.

Chapter 8

The wind was blowing, and the snow was riding the wind to faraway lands. I was caught in a blizzard, and even though the snow was cold, the wind hit me like a ray of heat. I held up the bottle of sparkling water that the old man had given me. I supposed it was a good thing that this tundra was so warm. If it were cold, then the water might freeze, and I wouldn't be able to use it. Though I'm still not so sure I should use it. All I have is the word of an old, dying man. Who knows what this water will do to me if I drink it?

I started to feel a cold draft down the back of my neck. At first, I thought nothing of it. But after some more thought, I realized that the draft was cold ... in a warm environment.

Slowly, I crept my gaze over my shoulder and saw a furry, white wolf that was the size of a polar bear. It stared at me intensely with bluish-purple eyes that twinkled as if reflecting a starry sky. I'd seen this thing before when I was talking to that old man. I thought I had seen something out of the corner of my eye, but it wasn't a bear, it was this giant wolf. Maybe this was what attacked the man in the first place ... and now it's come for me.

It stepped toward me, exhaling snowflakes from its nostrils. I stepped backward, quickly looking behind and then back at the wolf, trying to get a better sense of my surroundings. It was only a quick glance, so I wasn't certain, but I thought I saw some ice buildings I could hide in. The beast was inching closer and closer, and it bared obsidian black teeth. I had to make a decision, and it was one of the easiest decisions I've ever made. Run!

I headed for an ice building, looking for cover, but the wolf was chasing me, and gaining. It pounced into the air and landed atop the ice building I was heading for. The force of the icy debris that hit me when it shattered knocked me to the ground.

The wolf growled, and I searched around for something I could use to defend myself. Then I saw the bottle of sparkling water next to me. I must have dropped it. Picking it up, I debated whether I should drink it. I held it up, and it glistened and sparkled like the snow around me. But through it, I could see the giant white wolf readying its paw. I ducked as it swiped at me, but the force of the impact of its paw hitting the snow pushed me back into the wall of another ice building. I rubbed my arm, as it took the brunt of the collision. It would probably ache for a few days ...

The bottle of sparkling water was still in my hand. Now that I think about it, the water really is my only hope here.

There's no way I'll escape this wolf. If the water is poisonous, I was dead anyway, but if it's not …

I opened the bottle and downed the whole thing with just a few gulps, and as I watched the wolf inch toward me again, I felt different. I felt alert, energized, as if I could carry the entire planet on my shoulders or something crazy like that.

The wolf pounced and swiped at me again, but this time, I dodged, and the force of the impact did not push me back. It was working. The wolf swiped at me again, and I caught its paw with my hand and punched it with my other hand. It whimpered, jumped back, and stared at me with its starry eyes. Then it lowered its head and slowly limped away.

I did it. I beat it. I fought off a giant alien wolf. This water is amazing! I feel strong, empowered, like nothing can hurt me. I had to find more. The old man was right; I wouldn't survive without it. I don't even know how long the effects last. There was a tall, snowy mountain in the distance, the perfect place to look for more.

I ran, and what a run it was. I had to have been running three times faster than usual, and I wasn't even breaking a sweat, despite the warm weather. I felt like an athlete, like one of those muscular action heroes. I was unstoppable.

I made it to the foot of the mountain and started climbing. I wasn't out of breath, I wasn't tired; the cold snow didn't bother my fingers, and the warm winds didn't make me sweat. Only some parts of the mountain were steep, so I climbed up those parts and hiked up others. And with a combination of those two methods, I quickly made it to the summit—and when I say quickly, I mean like a gecko scurrying up a wall. That fast.

Atop the mountain, I could see far out into the distance. The biomes on this planet were very small. Beyond the tundra I was in, I could see the desert I met Skylar in, a dense forest, a stony wasteland, and lots of little cabins scattered around. It was like this whole planet was just a patchwork of other planets.

I couldn't see any springs of sparkling water, but I did notice something strange beside me. There was a circle of palm trees, and within that circle, there was a little pond of water … and it was sparkling. I grinned. That was a lot easier to find than I thought, but I guess that old man had to have gotten his supply from somewhere. He probably got it from here.

I entered the circle of trees. From within, it resembled a hot and humid rainforest, but it felt like a dry, winter snowstorm. I could see my own breath as I shivered. I was feeling the temperature again. I wonder if the water's effects are starting to wear off. I dipped my finger into the pond. Despite the cold weather, the pond wasn't frozen. It actually felt quite warm. What an odd planet this was. I couldn't even begin to make sense of it.

I opened my empty bottle and filled it with the sparkling water from the pond. Holding the now-filled bottle up to get a better look at it, I noticed something odd. The water in the bottle wasn't sparkling, yet the water in the pond was. The water I got from the old man sparkled in the bottle, so this water couldn't be what I was looking for. But then, what was making the water in the pond sparkle? I dipped my hand in and waved the pond water around, making ripples. The sparkles rippled also; it was a reflection. Looking up, I realized that the sky was full of twinkling stars. All of them glistened so beautifully, like a starry night back on Earth. I don't remember it being nighttime outside of this little rainforest. Yet another thing that didn't make any sense.

I sipped some of the water in my bottle; it was fresh, not salty. I decided to keep it. Water will always come in handy.

As I closed the bottle, my gaze went to the worn bracelet I was wearing. I had drunk the whole bottle of sparkling water, and I felt fine. No madness. Is that because I was wearing this? Everything else the old man said has been right so far, so maybe I should keep it on, just in case.

I suddenly felt drained, fatigued. The water's effects must have fully worn off. It felt a lot colder now. I wish I hadn't drunk all the water; I still have a huge mountain to climb down from. Great. I wonder if the amount I drank is related to how long the effects last. That's a good question, but I'll never answer it now, not until I find more sparkling water. Besides, I have to figure out how to get down this mountain.

I exited the palm tree circle and returned to the warm snowstorm. As I looked down the side of the mountain, my heart sank to my stomach. When I was coming up here, I didn't realize how tall it was. I took a deep breath and started climbing.

Without the sparkling water's assistance, I quickly lost my balance. I tumbled down the snowy mountain, gradually picking up speed until the ground beneath me caved in, and I fell.

It was a rough landing, but nothing was broken, just a few bruises. It seemed like I was in some sort of cave. It was dark, but the light that came in from where I'd fallen illuminated one thing more than anything else: a little pool of sparkling water.

I rushed over, crouched next to it, cupped the water in my hands, and drank. This was it. I already felt more energized, and my bruises didn't ache anymore. I knew that old man had to have gotten his supply from somewhere nearby. I'm just glad I found it. I don't think I would have been able to get out of this cave without it. I certainly couldn't jump out of the hole I fell through with just my regular jumping ability.

I sat up against the wall of the cave and yawned. I guess it had been a long day. This cave should be safe enough to sleep in.

It didn't take long for my eyelids to droop and for me to fall asleep. But before I drifted off entirely, an image appeared in my mind ... words ...

FIRST EVENT
STORM

Chapter 9

My eyes tore open and sweat dripped down my face. It was hot, boiling. There wasn't as much light coming through the hole at the top of the cave as there was before. There was a ton of snow coming through, though. Had the storm gotten worse?

I paused. That word. Storm. Why does that seem familiar? I can't remember. I'm sure I heard someone say it, or maybe ... I saw it somewhere.

I stroked my hand across my forehead and wiped away the sweat. Then I opened my bottle of fresh water and swallowed its entire contents within seconds. It didn't help much; I was still burning.

It was too hot to stay here; it felt like a sauna. I scrambled over to the pool of sparkling water and filled my bottle with it. Then I drowned my face in the pool and drank as much as I could. The heat was already feeling more tolerable. I placed the bottle in my satchel for safekeeping, and with the power bestowed upon me by the sparkling water, I leaped through the hole and out of the cave.

Now I was outside, I could see that this was definitely a storm, the hottest blizzard I'd ever experienced. The snow evaporated the second it touched down, revealing the tundra's purple grassy hills that were once covered in snow. I wasn't even sure how it could be snowing in such sweltering heat. The misty purple sky was blocked out by billowing grey clouds, and the wind blew violently. I could hear what I guessed were avalanches in the distance, but I could barely see anything. The snow, the clouds—they made everything hazy. I could just about see a few metres ahead.

I sighed. I had to start moving before the sparkling water wore off. Maybe I could find someplace cooler. I wiped the sweat from my brow and started on my way.

***

I had travelled far past the tundra and into a rainforest. The temperature wasn't as hot here, but the storm was still going. I couldn't escape it. No matter how far I travelled, the storm raged on. And the effects of the storm appeared to be different depending on where you were. In the tundra, it was a snowy blizzard, but in this rainforest, it's a thunderstorm. Lightning shot down from the grey sky (though, I suppose lightning technically shoots upward). Even still, I could hear trees cracking and falling around me, so I was fully focused on finding a way out of here. Tall trees are a terrible thing to be around in this kind of storm. I sipped my sparkling water incrementally, attempting to maintain its effects continuously. Otherwise, I'd find it much harder to walk in these strong winds.

"Help!" I heard someone call. "Help me, please."

I tried to follow the sound of the voice, but it was a little difficult to home in on it with all the wind distorting the sound.

"Hello?" I called.

"Please, help," came the voice again. "I think my leg is broken."

"Hang on, I'm on my way. Keep yelling so I can find you."

Though it was difficult, I did eventually find where the voice was coming from. It was a man, albeit one with scales rather than skin. His leg was trapped under a fallen tree trunk.

His teeth were gritted, and his face was all scrunched up. "Please, I can't take the pain."

"Hang on."

I sipped some more sparkling water and placed my hands firmly underneath the tree trunk. Taking a deep breath, I lifted. Even with the water's help, the tree was heavy, but I couldn't drop it now. The fact that it was raining didn't make things any easier. The tree was soaked in rainwater, making it heavier and slipperier. I glanced at the man's leg; it was approaching full deformity with how mangled it was. I couldn't ask him to move it. I had to move the tree away from him.

I took a quick breath in and gave one big push, launching the tree about a metre away. It landed with a huge thud, and I covered my ears to dampen the sound.

I took a second to catch my breath. I couldn't believe I'd just done that. This water was incredible.

"Thank you," the man said.

"No problem. Give me your hand. I'll help you up."

I got him to his feet and let him use my body for support. I'm not usually one for touching—and believe me, I feel very uncomfortable right now—but there was a storm raging out here, and I had to help this man get to safety.

"I don't suppose you know of a safe place where I can take you?" I asked him.

He pointed forward with a shaky hand. "That way, due west. There's a house of doctors. Stumbled across it a few days ago. They can help me."

I started in that direction. "How do you know this is west?" I asked.

"I don't know. It feels like west. Do you not get that?"

"What, a feeling for what direction I'm heading? No."

He looked at me. "Oh, right ... I guess you wouldn't ... No scales."

"Wait, you can feel the compass directions with your scales?"

He mumbled something incoherently. He was running low.

"Hey, stay alert," I urged him. "I'll get you there soon."

***

After a bit of walking, we arrived at a wooden cabin. Multiple lights mounted near its roof were illuminating the area, and there was a sign next to the door with a red cross on it, like the first-aid symbol back on Earth. I wondered if the symbol was being universally translated, the same way everyone's speech was being translated. I doubt every planet's first-aid symbol is a red cross. If that's the case, that must mean everyone's brains have been altered somehow so we can all understand each other, languages and symbols. I wonder why.

"Is this the place?" I asked the man, brushing back my soaking wet hair to stop it from falling into my line of sight.

His response was delayed. I guessed he was trying to muster up the energy to speak. "Yes ... this is the place."

His breathing was shallow. I got the feeling that something else was wrong with him. Maybe he was sick before having gotten caught under that tree.

I quickly helped the man into the cabin. It was much bigger on the inside than it appeared from the outside, although, that was probably due to the interior layout. We were in a large central room that connected to many other rooms in the back of the cabin. There were people everywhere, all of whom were visibly ill. All, that is, except for one: a small boy who was speaking to a woman with a red, sniffly nose.

"Now, you should be fine in a bit," said the young boy as he handed the woman a paper bag. "Just make sure that you cough into this. You're contagious, and I can't have you infecting everyone here."

The boy noticed me and approached. "Hello. Can I help you lot?" I noticed he had an English accent. Well, it sounded English, at least. Not only did everyone speak the same language here, but there were also Earth accents here, too. How strange.

"You look in a bad way," he said to the man I was helping. "You here for medical aid?"

I answered for the man, as he didn't seem to have the energy to speak. "I found him pinned under a tree. Is there a doctor around who can help him?"

"That would be me."

I took a good look at him—his short, black hair; his tanned, hairless face; and his small, grubby hands. He was a little kid; he couldn't have been a doctor. Although, he was wearing what looked like a stethoscope around his neck.

"How old are you?" I questioned.

"Nine years young."

"Nine years? And you're a doctor?"

"Do you need my help or not? I don't know why everyone here questions my credentials, but I'm a busy boy."

"Um ... yeah, sorry." I presented the man to him.

"I see." He walked around, eyeballing the man's leg from multiple angles. Then he abruptly yelled, "Cassie, bring me a contract!"

I subtly covered my ears to dampen the sound of the yell.

A tiny girl with neon red-orange hair feverishly emerged from one of the backrooms with a metal cart overflowing with various items.

"Here you are, doctor," she said, handing the boy a sheet of paper and a clipboard. It sounded like she had an Irish accent.

"Thank you, Cassie." The boy presented the contract to the man I was helping. "Right, before I fix your leg and give you a quick check-up, I'll need you to sign this contract stating that any land you currently own and/or will own in the future belong to me." He held out a pen, which he retrieved from his pocket.

The man slowly reached out his shaky hand, took the pen, and signed.

"Good," said the boy, taking back the pen and contract. "Now that that's sorted, Cassie, sort his leg out please."

"Certainly, doctor." The little girl fumbled around her cart and found a syringe. She filled it with some sort of yellow fluid and then stuck the needle into the man's leg. The man scrunched up his face when she did so.

"Now, just walk around for a bit, and your leg should be fine," the boy reassured.

"Okay. Thanks, doc," said the man. He looked at me. "And thank you for getting me here."

"Don't mention it," I said.

He started walking around. He didn't even need my help anymore.

"Are you sure he should be walking?" I asked the boy.

"Of course I'm sure."

"But shouldn't you give him a cast or something?"

He laughed. "What for?"

"Don't worry, mister, he'll be fine," Cassie butt in. "The drug I injected him with is very versatile."

The man walked back over to us. "Thank you, doc," he said. "I feel great."

"I'm sure you do. I still need to give you the once over, though, so if you wouldn't mind popping into one of the backrooms. Cassie?"

"Uh, Room ... C is free, doctor."

He looked at her. "You don't sound so sure."

"Well, what do you expect, doctor? There are a lot of fecking people around, and I'm just trying to keep everything straight. Room C is available."

"All right, you heard the girl," said the doctor to the man. "Pop into Room C for us, and we'll look you over in a bit."

As the man bowed to us and took his leave, another man entered the cabin and feverishly made his way to the young doctor.

"Doc, you've got to help me," he spluttered.

"Cassie, contract."

"Of course, doctor." Cassie fished around her metal cart for another contract and handed it to him.

"You'll need to sign this before we help you." He presented his contract to the man.

"What is it?" the man asked.

"A contract stipulating that all land currently owned by you and/or land that you will come to own in the future belong to me."

"What? I ain't signing that. A place to live is one of the best things you can have on this planet."

"Sorry," I interjected. "I don't understand. You own property here?"

The man looked at me. "Uh, not exactly. I live in a place, and I call it mine, but there ain't nothing saying it's mine per se."

"So you just found a place to live here?"

"Yeah, they're scattered everywhere—cabins, just like this one here. It's kind of strange actually. I wonder who built—Ah! My head!" He cupped his hands to his forehead.

The doctor retrieved a card-shaped object from his pocket and held it up to his eye, angling it toward the man's head.

"You've got a brain tumour," he said. "A massive one at that."

"What?" the man blurted. "No. No, you've got to get it out."

"Sign my contract." He presented the man with a pen.

"Is that all you care about, taking people's property?"

"As it happens, yes."

"The doctor has a very versatile skill set," commented Cassie. "He can't work for free."

The man hesitated. "Man, you kids are crooks. Give me the contract; it's not like you can police it anyway."

"I wouldn't be too certain of that." The doctor smiled.

"What's that supposed to mean?" the man questioned, although this didn't seem to sway his decision; he signed the contract anyway.

"Thank you for your cooperation," said the doctor, taking back the contract and handing it to Cassie, who then put it in the metal cart. "If I were you, I wouldn't break my contract. I think you'll find it's very enforceable. Cassie, I'll need a boost."

"Yes, doctor." Cassie knelt down in front of the young doctor, and he climbed atop her shoulders.

"Remove your hands from your head, please," the doctor said, and the man complied. He then began massaging multiple parts of the man's face and neck. "Raise your left arm, please." Again, the man did as he was told. The doctor began massaging the raised arm, too.

When he was finished, he climbed down from Cassie's shoulders and said, "All right. Your tumour has now started the shrinking process. It will be gone by tomorrow."

"Are you sure?" the man asked.

"Absolutely positive. But if you still have a headache tomorrow (which you won't) just come back, and I'll give you another treatment."

"Okay. Thanks. You're a lifesaver." The man waved to him and left.

"How did you do that?" I asked the doctor.

"Do what?" He straightened up his shirt.

"Cure his tumour."

"I massaged his pressure points. Couldn't you tell? You were the one gawking at me with that stupid face of yours."

"Doctor, that's rude," said Cassie quickly.

The doctor rolled his eyes. "Sorry. I'm sure your countenance is very aesthetically pleasing wherever you're from."

I ignored the insult. I was so astonished by everything he was doing. "So, you cured a broken leg with an injection, and you cured a brain tumour with a massage?"

"Yes," he laughed. "Why do you sound so amazed? It's not like a brain tumour and a broken leg qualify as medical emergencies."

"If those aren't medical emergencies, then what is?"

Something behind me drew the doctor's attention. "*That* is a medical emergency. Excuse me." He ran over to help a woman who had just stumbled in. Cassie followed him urgently with her cart.

The woman had some sort of pinkish vine growing out of her head.

"Oi, question man," the doctor called, looking my way.

"Are you talking to me?" I asked.

"Is there someone else here asking me a million questions? Come on, I need your help."

I walked over to him, and when close enough, I noticed the vine coming from the woman's head was moving, swaying back and forth very subtly. And the woman was staring into space, barely aware of what was happening.

"I need you to hold her up," the doctor said to me. "She's almost fully lost control of her body."

I clenched up slightly. I didn't really want to touch her, but I did so anyway.

"Cassie, prep the needle, will you?"

"Yes, doctor." Cassie nodded and dove her head into her cart.

"Um ... what is growing out of this woman's head?" I asked.

"A fungus," the doctor answered. "Specifically, Ophiocordyceps unilateralis?"

"You mean that fungus that turns ants into zombies?"

"That depends. What's an ant?"

"It's an insect. They live in colonies underground."

"Okay, then yeah, that's the one. Cordyceps, that's what's growing out of this woman's head, and if we're not quick, it will spew us all with its spores; and we'll be infected and find warm and humid places at which we will hang from the highest point we can reach until we die of malnourishment. It's quite a brutal way to go actually."

"But cordyceps can only affect insects. They can't survive in higher body temperatures."

He laughed. "You are so naïve; I love it. It's evolution. One day cordyceps is infecting insects, the next day, that doesn't cut it anymore, so it moves on to people."

"The needle's prepped, doctor," Cassie interrupted.

"Great. Prick her."

"Right away, doctor." Cassie immediately injected the woman with a bright pink fluid, and the woman's skin became cold and hard in response.

"Take her to the back, please, will you, Cassie?"

Cassie looked up at me. "I'll take her off your hands, mister." I passed the frozen woman over to her, and she took her by the hand and dragged her to the backroom like an old, rolled-up rug. The woman didn't make a sound; she was like a frozen statue.

"That'll be a long surgery to look forward to," the doctor grumbled to himself. "Hopefully she'll sign my contract when we're done, otherwise this will have all been a massive waste of time."

"What is it with you and contracts?" I asked.

"Well, I'm not giving my services away, am I? Since there's no money on this planet, I need a different type of currency. Property works the same way money does; the more you have, the more powerful you are."

"But you can't possibly enforce that."

"Sure I can. If someone breaks my contract, they'll be tormented by Cotraxyi for the rest of their sorry life."

"Who?"

"Cotraxyi. It's a scythe-wielding spirit in a cloak who polices all contracts written on Cotraxyium paper. If anyone breaks the bonds of one of these contracts, they will be taken to another world and tormented by their worst fears until they die of natural causes. Either way, I get what I want."

"You don't really believe that, do you?"

"I've seen it happen, and it can happen again if people try to receive my services without payment."

I stared at his tiny stature. "I don't understand. You're only nine years old; how can you do all this medical stuff?"

"Years of experience." He grinned.

"What, five years?"

He laughed. "Five? Try fifty."

"Fifty? I thought you said you were nine years old."

"No, I said I was nine years *young*. I was born at seventy-two years young."

"So you're ... growing younger?"

"Is that strange to you?"

"Yes, very."

He shook his head and smiled. "I was nineteen before I got to this planet, just on the bookend of my prime years. I was getting ready to retire and then—poof—I'm here. There are so many sick and injured on this planet, and offering my services is the best way I know to be well off here—get in good with the people, get rich with property—but I'm definitely getting too young for this job. I'm already too short to reach the things I used to be able to reach, and in just a few years, I'll lose the ability to walk and talk. And Cassie is younger than I am, so I won't have her around to help for long. I'd like to just get off this planet so I can retire properly, you know? Say, what planet are you from?"

"Uh, Earth."

"Whereabouts is that?"

"The Milky Way."

"No, no, on the Intergalactic Map."

"The what?"

He sighed. "You're from one of *those* planets, aren't you? This all must be terrifying for you, then. Is your planet at least medically skilled?"

"What do you mean?"

"Have you cured cancer yet?"

"Not exactly."

"What about the common cold?"

"We have remedies for it, but we haven't actually cured it." I felt a little like an ambassador for planet Earth who was just starting to realize how far behind we are compared to other planets.

"Hmm." He rubbed his nose. "If we ever do make it back to our own planets, I would advise you to work on curing the common cold. It may not seem too pressing at first, but you'd be surprised how much better off you'll be once it's gone."

This was so weird. I was talking to a nine-year-old who knew more than any doctor I've ever met.

"Anyway," he said. "I have a surgery to get to before we all turn into fungus zombies. I trust you can see yourself out."

I nodded.

"I'm Trevor, by the way." He offered me a handshake.

"I'm Charles," I responded, but I didn't shake his hand.

"What's the matter, don't want to shake my hand?"

"Sorry, I'm just not a handshaking person."

"Oh, all right, then. I'll try not to be offended."

"Oh, no, I don't mean to offend you."

"I'm joking," he laughed. "They don't have sarcasm on your planet?"

"No, they do," I said quietly.

He smiled. "You're an odd one, aren't you?"

He walked away before I could answer, heading for the backrooms. But before he made it there, a woman started coughing violently.

"Oi, you!" the doctor screamed. "In the bag! In the bag! What don't you understand about the word *contagious*? I told you before, cough in the bag. Bloody hell!"

I grinned slightly and took my leave.

Chapter 10

I had been walking for a while now, but the scenery hadn't changed much. I think I was out of the rainforest because there were fewer trees than before, but that's not to say the trees were entirely absent. This could have just been a less-wooded part of the same forest.

The storm had come and gone, and the only traces it left were the scorch marks on the ground from the lightning strikes, and the fallen trees and other structures. I was lucky enough to find a pool of sparkling water on my travels, though, and I topped up my supply there.

I just kept travelling. No matter what happens, I just keep walking. Ever since I arrived on this planet, I've been a wanderer. I don't even know where I'm going. It seems that everyone I meet has a plan or some inkling of what they should do here. That doctor, Trevor, he's using his abilities to gain more land and power, and at the same time, he's helping people in need. Skylar and his group are just trying to help people, too, and get everyone off this planet. And me, what am I doing? I opted out of staying with Skylar; I can never seem to stay in one place. Why is that? Maybe I feel disconnected from everyone. I wasn't used to having friends on Earth, maybe I'm subconsciously trying to remain a loner here ... because it's familiar. Although, there was that one girl I met ... Angela. I wonder how she's doing. I wonder if she's upset that I missed the movie we were meant to see. Or maybe she's angry.

"Excuse me! Sorry! Out of the way!" The voice immediately ripped my thoughts away, and I was pushed to the ground.

The culprit was a feverish-looking man wearing a long brown coat and a rather shiny wristwatch.

"Sorry," he said quickly. "I didn't mean to push you." He offered a hand to help me up, but I refused it and got up on my own.

Then he suddenly cried out and wrapped his arms around his stomach.

"Are you okay?" I asked, my hands covering my ears.

"I will be." His eyes darted around like he was looking for something. "Yes, I'll be fine. I just need to find ... There!" He pointed a long finger into the distance, at a small body of water.

"You need ... water?" I questioned, finding it hard to believe that all this commotion was just because he was thirsty.

"Hold these, would you?" The man undressed and handed me his clothing.

Before I had the chance to object, I was holding his full attire, and he dashed into the water completely naked. Once fully submerged, a yellow gas seeped out of the water, and then the man's head popped out, and that same gas seeped out of his mouth as well.

When the gas had fully dispersed, the man trudged out of the water and over to me. I covered my eyes, not wanting to see his naked body.

"You see? Absolutely nothing to worry about," he said. "Just an energy-worm. Like a tapeworm, but instead of eating the food you eat, they eat the energy you have, slowly, until you can't go on. But they have a fundamentally fascinating fatal flaw: water. Quite ironic actually. The thing that sustains life for many lifeforms is also the very same thing that can take it away from an energy-worm. Once I was fully submerged in the water, that worm was altogether, absolutely, assuredly abolished."

"You're naked," I said, as it was the only thing on my mind.

"So I am."

"Just ... here." I handed back his clothes, and he got dressed.

As soon as he'd gotten his long coat back on and popped the collar, he sat down by a tree, claiming that the energy-worm had drained him and he needed to rest. He didn't seem very tired to me, though.

I stood next to him, as I didn't feel like sitting.

"Are you hungry?" he asked.

"A little, I guess. But I don't think there's any food nearby, unless you've got some on you."

The man scrunched up his nose, and it turned into a dog's snout. He used it to sniff around. "In the trees. You can't see them, but I smell apples somewhere. I'll be right back." He removed his shoes, and his hands and feet became like those of a gecko, though they were proportional to his size. He climbed up the tree just like a lizard would, and I lost him in all the leaves.

I blinked a few times, wondering if that had actually happened.

The man jumped down from the tree seconds later, landing on his cat paws. "Here you are. Freshly picked." He handed me one of his two apples, and then he sat back down against the tree and began to eat the other one.

"Thanks," I said, taking a bite out of my apple. "How did you do that?"

"Do what? Oh, yes, the gecko-hands thing."

I nodded.

"I'm a shapeshifter. Anything I've ever seen, anything at all, I can mimic in any part of my body."

"You're a shapeshifter? Like, not just camouflaging your skin but actually changing your whole physiology?"

"Yes, I'm a sincerely savvy shapeshifter, sometimes secretly. And a time traveller. Well, I suppose I was born a shapeshifter. But I time travel enough to consider that part of my identity as well ... I'm a time traveller by occupation and a shapeshifter by physiology. Yes, that makes sense." He pointed to his shiny wristwatch. "And this is my trusty time machine."

I eyed his very ordinary-looking wristwatch. "That's a time machine?"

"Yep. There's a black hole inside of it, very powerful. It sucks in absolutely everything, including time. It can bend it like an element and make it malleable, and essentially, I am able to put the past into my future. It's also a teleportation device. You know, time travel without space travel is a bit pointless, so ..."

"Whoa, back up. There's a black hole inside your wristwatch?"

"Yes. The watch is actually a lot larger on the inside than it is on the outside. There's a whole universe in here."

"Really?"

"No, of course not. Could you imagine? No, the black hole is just small, tiny, the size of a pinprick. It does its job, though."

"Wait, hold on, what stops the black hole from sucking up the watch and you along with it?"

"Well, the interior is coated in dark matter, which stops everything else from getting sucked in."

I scratched my head. "But then, how does it suck in time if the dark matter stops it from sucking in everything?"

"Look, it's cataclysmically complicated and a lot to go through. All you need to know is that it works."

There was a short silence as he fiddled around with his watch, but I broke it quickly. "So, what's a shapeshifting time traveller doing on this planet anyway? You're probably the only person here who doesn't have to be. You can go to some other time before any of this Planet-of-Shadows stuff happened."

"Why would I leave? This is one of the greatest events in history. You see, I'm a simple man, just someone who wants to know. I want to see all the things the universe has to offer. There are one hundred people here from fifty different planets, all gathered with just one goal: survival. It's a remarkable thing to spectate."

"Spectate? Is this a game to—"

"Wait! Hold on! Shut up, shut up, shush for a second." He rocketed to his feet and stared at me with huge, dilated eyes. They almost looked like eagle eyes, and knowing that he was a shapeshifter, they probably were eagle eyes. He was making me uncomfortable.

"I know you," he said, snapping his fingers repeatedly. "I'm meant to tell you something. You're Alex, right?"

"Uh ... no."

"Oh ... Then you know someone named Alex."

"No, I don't."

"Hmm ... I must have the timelines mixed up. Come on, come on, get it together!" He banged his hands on his forehead violently. "I thought I was getting better. I got my mind almost completely wiped a little while ago—unsafe travel, dangerous but necessary. But I thought ... Okay, I think I have this right. You will know someone named Alex at some point. And your meeting him, plus a few others, is imminently important. But in order for any of that to happen, I'm supposed to say something. I must have it written down." He pulled out a book with a black leather cover from the inside pocket of his jacket. "What year is it on your planet?"

"2016," I said cautiously. "Or it was when I was there. I guess it's 2026 now."

"All right. In that case, my name's Tom."

"I'm Charles."

"Yes, I know."

"You didn't before. Two seconds ago, you thought my name was Alex."

"Because I had the timelines all muddled up. I know what I'm saying now."

"And wait, why did you ask me for the year?"

"I have a different name and face for different time periods. It's so I can't be easily recognized."

"What's wrong with being recognized?"

He stopped looking in his book and stared at me. "Come now, Charles, you're smarter than that. If I'm recognized in timelines that are too far apart from each other, could you imagine the coalescence of chronicled calamities that would commence? Madam Time does not like her work tampered with, I can tell you that."

"Madam Time? Who's she?"

"Well, she's not a *she* per se; that's just how people tend to think of her. She's the embodiment of time; she controls it, and she is it. But you don't want to get on her bad side. She and the oth—" He suddenly collapsed back to the ground, crying out and clutching his chest.

"What's wrong? Are you okay?"

"Huh?" He looked up at me. "Oh, yeah, I'm fine. I just carried this conversation on for another five minutes and realized I still hadn't said what I was supposed to say. So, I travelled back five minutes into the past to start over."

"Wait a minute," I objected. "If you travelled back in time, into your own timeline, shouldn't there now be two of you here?"

"Ah, there he is. That's the intelligent Charles McCoy I know ... even if you're wrong. Theoretically, you're correct, there should be two of me. But in reality, Madam Time doesn't like two of the same person being in the same timeline together, so she kills off the newer one ... or the older one ... um, the one who's youngest. Though, I think I've figured out a way to get around that, but that's a story for another time. Let's stay on track here. I travelled back in time and now occupy the same space as past me once did, and so my past self was chronologically killed and that was the pain I just felt. I just died ... and it was very painful."

I blinked a few times. "Uh, okay, sure. Tell me what you had to tell me."

"What? Oh, right, I nearly forgot again." He leafed through his book. "Let's see ... Ah! Here we are. I am meant to say that the Planet of Shadows was created by a shadow-dweller, and The Events exist to test the adaptability of the people here. However, in order to begin one of The Events, the shadow-dweller must leave its sanctuary and go to the planet's surface to set it up. It always goes to the same spot. I'm not sure where because it seems I neglected to write that information down, but if you ever want to get off this planet, you'll need to find out where that shadow-dweller goes. Oh, and you must do this before The Third Event. Despite what you've been told, they have no intention of letting any of you leave. Once The Third Event occurs, everything dies."

I swallowed. "What events? What's a shadow-dweller? What are you talking about?"

"You'll find out soon enough. Hopefully, I've successfully nudged you in the right direction. I really don't want to go back into my own timeline again." He sighed.

I waited a second and then said, "I guess what you said worked."

"How do you figure?"

"Well, if it didn't, you'd have come back from the future again to start over, right?"

"No, it doesn't work that way. If I were to go back into my own timeline again, you wouldn't know about it."

"But I knew about it the first time you did it."

"Because I came to talk to you. If I go back in time again now, I'd be doing so to talk to past you, not present you."

"But then wouldn't I remember you having gone back in time?"

"No, no, you don't … it doesn't … you know what, it's cumbersome, convoluted, and catastrophically, cataclysmically complicated. Let's just leave it at that."

"Agreed." I smiled.

"Anyway, I have places to be." He started fiddling with his wristwatch. "It was nice to meet you, Charles … or I suppose it was nice to see you again. Though, I don't fully remember meeting you the first time. But I must have done because how else would I know who you are …?"

While he mumbled to himself, his skin started to sparkle. Then he disappeared.

Chapter 11

There wasn't a tree in sight; everything was just a flat sandy desert. This planet seemed to be full of deserts and forests; it was a rarity to find anything else. I wonder if there's a reason for that. I wonder if there's a reason for anything that goes on here. All that stuff that Tom talked about—The Events, something called a "shadow-dweller"—The Events sounded vaguely familiar, though I couldn't figure out why, but the shadow-dweller, I don't know what that is.

In the distance, a small bump poked out from the otherwise flat horizon. As I got closer, I realized the bump was a middle-aged woman with dark skin and a huge afro. She was sitting on the ground, staring around. Maybe she was nervous. She looked human, but then, so did Tom before I found out he was a shapeshifter.

"Are you okay?" I called out to her when I was within her earshot.

"Get away!" she yelled. "Stay away from the holes."

"Holes? What holes?"

My eyes shot downward, in search of these holes, and sure enough, there were holes scattered all over the ground. They were fairly large, maybe four or five metres across, but I didn't notice them before because they were covered in sand. They looked more like circular indentations than holes. I wonder why the woman wants me to stay away.

My question was immediately answered when one of the holes exploded in a plume of smoke and sand, and from it emerged a large, scaly serpent. It drifted upward, becoming airborne, yet it didn't have any wings. It had tiny forearms—proportionally, that is; its forearms were technically larger than me—and it had no hind legs. Its long, tube-like body ended in a fin, like the tailfin of a fish. When its black eyes looked back into my terrified ones, it opened its mouth, revealing a maw of neatly arranged, sharp teeth. At the same time, ears unfolded from the sides of its head—they were little and thin, kind of like bat wings.

Some sort of blue mist seeped out of its mouth, and then it shot out a blue beam. I narrowly avoided it, feeling its chilling cold graze my face. The beam struck the sand and froze it instantly.

The woman called out again. "Come to us, quickly!"

I had to mull her words over for a second. First, she wanted me to stay away, and now she wanted me to go to her. Well, technically, she said, "come to *us*". That's probably just another grammatical difference from whatever language she speaks on her planet.

The flying serpent unleashed a high-pitched squeal, and I decided to do as the woman said. I started running and almost tripped when another freezing cold blast crashed down behind me, but I made it to where the woman was, and when I did, the serpent plummeted back into one of the holes.

"Are you all right?" I asked, crouching down next to her.

"Fine," she responded quickly. "Stay close to us, away from the holes."

When she said this, I realized that there were no holes where she sat. The holes were all around us, but not in this one spot. It was like we were in the centre of a doughnut, and the holes were the sprinkles.

I quickly sat next to her. Being near people wasn't particularly within my comfort zone, especially if it was someone I'd only just met, but in this case, I was willing to make an exception.

There was another explosion, and the serpent re-emerged from a hole. Its black eyes spotted us, and it slithered through the sandy, airborne smoke. But then it stopped and turned away when it came too close. For some reason, it didn't seem to be able to come near us, not as if something were stopping it, but as if it didn't want to.

"Why isn't it attacking?" I looked at the woman only with my head, as my eyes remained fixated on the serpent.

"From what we've gathered, the holes in the ground are an intricate tunnelling system, and they also double as visual territory markers. What's strange is that its territory seems to be ring-shaped, so because we are in the centre, it won't attack us; we're not technically in its territory. That's what we think, at least."

"I guess that makes sense," I agreed, taking my eyes off the serpent to look at her. "Who's *we*?"

"What do you mean?"

"You keep saying *we* or *us*. Who else is here?"

She smiled and pointed to herself. "*We* is us."

"Like ... you have a hive mind?"

"Of sorts."

"That is so cool."

The serpent plunged back into one of the holes.

"So now what?" I asked the woman.

"We don't know. This is as far as we've gotten."

"How long have you been here?"

"Maybe a few hours."

"We can't stay here forever. We have to deal with this thing and get out of here."

"Are you insane? We can't fight it; it shoots ice from its mouth."

I pulled the bottle of sparkling water from my satchel, took a sip, and then put the bottle back. "Don't worry. I can handle it."

As I ran into battle, I began to realize just how different I'd become. I've always shied away from confrontation, yet now I was ready to fight off a giant, ice-breathing serpent. Has my time on this planet changed me that much? Or maybe it's not the planet at all; maybe it's the water. I wouldn't dare fight this serpent without it. Have I grown a dependency on it; have I become addicted? Is that possible? No, it keeps me safe; I can't get addicted to it. That would be like getting addicted to wearing armour. Plus, I have the bracelet on. That stops the water from inflicting psychosis, and I don't feel psychotic, so it must be working ... But what if the bracelet doesn't stop the water from doing other things? What do I actually know about any of it? I just keep drinking the water without a second thought ... No. I'm overthinking it. The water keeps me safe. It makes me strong enough to fight the creatures on this planet. What is it they say about looking a gift horse in the mouth?

There was another explosion, and the serpent flew upward and dove straight for me. I leaped out of the way of an incoming beam of ice while trying to come up with a way to defeat it. How do you defeat an ice-breathing reptile? Reptiles don't do well in cold, but this one shoots ice, so it probably doesn't follow Earth reptile rules. What else can I try? The ice beam it shoots is pretty thin. I bet it comes out of a really tiny hole in its mouth, a hole that could be easily clogged. I avoided another ice beam, and when it hit the ground, it kicked up a huge plume of sand. That's it. I bet if I can get it to swallow enough sand, that'll clog it up enough for me and the woman to escape.

I grabbed a handful of desert sand and stood my ground. The serpent drifted over to me, slowly opening its mouth. I accounted for the wind resistance, and when the serpent was close enough, I threw the sand into its mouth, and it crashed to the ground, choking and coughing up shards of ice.

"Hurry," I yelled to the woman, "while it's distracted!"

She stood and ran toward me. When she caught up, we both dashed to the end of the serpent's territory, where the holes stopped. We were almost there, but the serpent had coughed up all the sand and was coming for us again.

"Keep going," I said to the woman while bending down to grab more sand.

I turned to face the serpent, and its mouth was already opened wide, preparing for another attack. But thanks to the sparkling water, I was quicker. I chucked the sand into its mouth, and it collapsed again, choking on its own icy breath. And that bought us enough time to escape the serpent's territory.

We stood outside the ring-shaped area and watched as the serpent coughed up all the sand and retreated back into one of the holes.

"How did you know that would work?" the woman asked.

"I didn't know it would work so well, but the beam the serpent was shooting was pretty small, so I figured it must have a really tiny throat or something, and it could be easily clogged."

She nodded. "You must be pretty smart."

"Um ... thanks, I guess."

"The water you drank, does that make you stronger?"

"Yeah, more or less. I found it on this planet. Apparently, without this bracelet I'm wearing, it will cause psychosis."

"How does the bracelet stop that?"

I stared at the brown leather around my wrist. "I ... have no clue."

There was a short silence that voiced my uncertainty better than words ever could.

The woman smiled at me. "Come with us."

"Where?"

"You seemed interested in our hive mind before, so we'll show you. Consider it a thank you for your help."

I smiled. "Okay."

She started walking. "We're Sandy, by the way."

I followed her. "I'm Charles."

***

We eventually arrived at a wooden cabin, the same sort as the other cabins that were scattered all over this planet. Sandy led me inside and shut the door behind us.

This cabin was furnished only with a bed. In the back of my mind, I'd been wondering why all these cabins were here, but what I should have been wondering was who furnishes them. Trevor's cabin was full of medical equipment, Skylar's cabin was like a little apartment, and this one only had a bed. Where's all this stuff coming from?

"We picked some berries the other day. Would you like some?" Sandy presented me with a basket of berries she retrieved from the corner of the room.

I took a handful of yellow ones. "Thanks."

"You're very welcome."

I bit into a berry; it was a little tangy but still nice. "Where did you get the berry basket?" I asked.

"On the bed. It was here when we found the cabin. Which reminds us ..." She stared at the bed. "It's okay; we can come out."

A humanoid figure with dimples in place of its eyes and mouth materialized on the bed. Skinny, pale, and dressed in white, the person floated atop the bed as if the air were water and they were adrift at sea.

"This is the other part of our mind," Sandy explained. The figure floated toward me as she continued to speak. "We are tethered through a psychic link. It's like an invisible leash—a rather long one, but even still, we can't be too far apart." It was Sandy talking, but it almost felt like the floating figure was doing the thinking.

"We come from a species that cannot speak," they continued. "We speak to our own kind telepathically, but not all creatures can speak as we do. One day, a race of aliens came to our world demanding to know if we had the element they were looking for. They were involved in a war we had no part in, and we didn't have what they wanted. But they were violent. They said their species had been deceived by a traveller, and they needed to find more of some element before their enemies destroyed them for leaving their world. They gave us a week to respond or else they would destroy all life on our planet. But we were unable to communicate with them; we needed an interpreter.

"We were sent to the nearest planet with intelligent life that could speak with voice. We established a psychic link with this woman and asked for help. We agreed and met up in an open field after calling our husband and saying goodbye to our son Alex."

"Alex?"

"Yes, Alex. Is that name odd on your planet?"

"No, it's just ... someone told me I would meet someone named Alex soon. I wonder if ..."

"That must be a different Alex. All that was so long ago; our Alex must be a grown man now. Probably working a fancy job in Neetro City." Sandy smiled.

"So how did you get here, then?"

The figure floated away from me and rested a hand on Sandy's shoulder. "When we returned to our planet with the interpreter, we found that the aliens had already destroyed everything. They had no intention of leaving us in peace.

"We no longer had need of an interpreter, so we started back for the planet the woman came from to return to our son. But when we arrived, a young woman met us there. She said her name was Samantha. And then she apologized because she explained that it was unlikely we would ever see Alex again. She said the aliens were coming for that world, too, and if they recognized us from the last planet, their attack would be worse. She gave us a golden ring and promised that if we put it on, she would watch over Alex and keep him safe."

"And you just believed her?" I questioned.

"Not entirely. But the ring was hard to resist; it called to us. And when we put it on, we ended up here."

"That's what happened to me. I found a golden ring on the ground, and it brought me here."

"We gather a similar sort of thing happened to everyone on this planet." The woman and the floating figure looked at each other. "We've made peace with the fact that we won't be going back. We just hope that, whoever that woman was, she keeps her word and watches over our boy."

We continued to talk for a bit, just weightless chitchat, and then I left. I had more questions than answers, a clear representation of just how little anyone knew about this planet, but I continued on still. That was all any of us could do.

Chapter 12

My travels had brought me to a dense forest. Unfortunately, the surrounding trees bared no fruit, and I was starving. Food quickly became the only thing I could think about, which was strange because I left Sandy's cabin only a few hours ago, and I ate there. Why was I so hungry now? I wonder if it's a side effect of the sparkling water. Or maybe it has to do with this forest. I don't know. I don't know how anything works on this planet. All I know is I'm starving. I need to find something to eat.

I stopped and paused for just a moment because I thought, in the corner of my eye, I could see a glimmer of red ... an apple! It was high up in a tree, but at that moment, elated by having even found something edible in the first place, I felt herculean. I felt like I could scale any tree, no water required. But I was wrong. That was made abundantly clear when my butt slid back down the tree trunk and crashed into the ground. It hurt, but I didn't break anything, except maybe my ego.

If I used the sparkling water, I could probably make it up the tree, but I didn't want to waste it. I need it to protect myself, in case I'm in danger. Though, I suppose the danger of starvation is a type of danger. I retrieved the bottle from my satchel and opened it, but before I could drink, a small, rat-like creature scurried up the tree and disappeared into the leaves. Before long, it scurried back down, holding the apple in its little front paws.

"Great," I muttered. "Now it's going to run off and eat *my* apple."

But it didn't run off. Instead, it looked at me with beady black eyes and held the apple up, seemingly offering it to me. It stared at me, blinking. Its huge, floppy ears moved up and down in tune with its breathing. It was cute. I took the apple and said thank you, although I doubted it understood English. Nevertheless, it curled up beside me as I sat against the tree and bit into the apple. It tasted just like an apple I could have gotten on Earth, and I wondered if it was an apple from Earth. After all, this planet is a patchwork of fifty different planets, including my own. Maybe this was something I was actually familiar with.

The rat-like creature nudged its tiny nose onto my lap, and I stroked its soft fur with my finger. I guess not every creature on this planet is inherently dangerous. Some of them are timid, docile, and just as lost as the rest of us.

It didn't take long for me to finish the apple, and now that I'd been satiated, I grew tired. The tiny creature I was stroking had fallen asleep, drooling all over my lap, and it wasn't long before I followed its example. But before I was fully asleep, at the exact moment I closed my eyes, words appeared in my head, and they read:

SECOND EVENT
QUAKE

Some time later, I awoke to a rumbling. The rat-like creature had disappeared, and for good reason; the ground was shaking so heavily I couldn't even stand. A cracking sound echoed throughout the forest. The ground was tearing open, dragging entire trees down. It was a fissure, and it was coming for me.

I quickly sipped my sparkling water; I didn't think I could walk on a ground this shaky without help. Slowly, I came to my feet and ran.

Even the trees far away from the fissure were tumbling down. A forest wasn't an ideal place to be in the middle of an earthquake. I had to find a way out of here. But I couldn't remember the way out of this forest, so I had to just pick a direction and run.

While I was running, I couldn't shake the feeling that I'd seen something about earthquakes before. Like a couple of words in a book, or maybe in a dream ... That's it! I remember. Before I fell asleep, I saw the words *Second Event Quake*. Didn't that time traveller say something about Events? I wonder if this is what he was talking about. And then, he said I had to do whatever I had to do before The Third Event. If this is The Second Event, I'm running out of time to figure this all out. I don't even remember The First Event. Did that already happen?

The coming of another fissure immediately halted my thoughts. I had to switch directions, but there was another fissure approaching from that direction, too. I was trapped. I couldn't climb the trees; the fissures would surely swallow them whole. And these fissures were huge; I couldn't jump far enough to leap over them. I didn't know what to do, but I supposed jumping was my best option. I didn't have high hopes, but maybe I could leap from the tops of the trees before they were swallowed up and escape that way. I took a breath and leaped.

I reached the top of a tree but slipped as it was swallowed into the ground. I fell with it, but I didn't fall all the way. Someone caught me. He stood at the edge of the fissure and held on to my hand, keeping me from plummeting below.

"Hold on," he said, and he hoisted me up to him and got me on relatively stable ground. "Follow me."

I did as he said and followed as he ran through the forest, weaving his way through the fissures and falling trees. He seemed a lot better than I was at navigating this earthquake.

I rubbed my hand on my pant leg, trying to get rid of the discomfort of his having touched me. I couldn't help but notice my saviour's long black coat; it stretched all the way down to his feet. The colour of the coat matched the colour of his hair and his two swords, which were sheathed and strapped to his back.

He stopped running suddenly and looked around. "Which way d'you think's out?"

"I thought you knew," I responded.

"I ain't talking to you."

I looked around. There was no one else here. "Then who are you talking to?"

He ignored me and looked to his right. "This way? You sure 'bout that? All right, man."

He dashed to the right. I followed and continued to examine his appearance. His hair was extremely spiky, and his features were exaggerated, almost like a real-life cartoon character. Or like he was on his way to an anime convention.

Before I knew it, he had successfully navigated us out of the forest and into a desert plain.

"And we're out." He smiled. "Stand back."

He drew his swords, which I now realized were katanas. He plunged them into the ground and a pink circle made out of strange foreign writing radiated outward from them. Then the earthquake stopped but only within the circle.

"What did you do?" I asked.

The man sat on the ground in the circle and pointed to the ground in front of him. "I set up a time circle," he answered. "As long as my blades are in the ground, all time is paused, save for living creatures, of course. That's against intergalactic law. You gonna sit?"

"Oh, right. Sorry." I sat on the ground in front of him.

"Name's Stryx, by the way."

"Charles."

He looked to his left for a moment and then back at me. "Well?"

"Well what?"

"Tri just asked you a question."

I cocked my head slightly. "Who's Tri?"

"Who d'you think?"

"I don't know; that's why I asked."

"Hey, man, I just saved your life. No need to be rude to Tri and Nine."

"Who's Nine?"

"Damn, you people are good at this."

"Good at what?"

"The ignoring thing. This is why I've gotta keep to myself. Most of the people here are chipped or something; you can hear all my thoughts. And every single one of you ignores my friends. Tri is the guy right beside me, black hair, triangular earrings. And Nine is the four-legged critter over here. It wouldn't kill you to at least say *hi*."

I looked around, but I didn't see anyone else here.

"Are you gonna answer the question?" Stryx continued.

"What question?"

"The one Tri just asked you."

I paused. "Uh ... what did Tri ask?"

"He asked where you're from."

"Oh. Okay. I'm from Earth. I doubt you'd know where that is."

"No, I think I've heard of it. Earth's the local name. You guys aren't intergalactic yet. Red planet, right?"

"Uh, no. It's next to a red planet, though."

"What, you mean that blue one with the puffy white stuff?"

"Yeah, that sounds right. I'm surprised you know it by the same name I do."

"Yeah, I read it in a textbook once. Earth's a protected planet."

"Have you been there?"

"Nope. I work for an interplanetary peacekeeping organization—the Tristan Corps, named after our late founder. Each of our members carries dual katanas. They're enchanted and designed to disperse evil thoughts."

"Has anyone from the Tristan Corps been to Earth? There's a ton of evil there."

"We don't deal with planets that ain't advanced enough to travel through space efficiently. You don't know about us, but we know about you, and knowing Earth, it's probably gonna stay that way for a bit." Stryx looked to his right. "I don't know. It shouldn't last too long. Although, I don't think this is a natural quake, so who can say?"

"What do you mean?" I asked, even though I didn't think he was talking to me.

"Quakes occur when tectonic plates crash into each other. This quake is only vibrating the surface of the planet."

"How do you know?"

"That's what my katanas are telling me, and they're the ones sticking out of the ground right now, so I'm inclined to believe 'em."

"But those fissures in the forest were way deeper than the surface of the planet."

"How would you know? This is your first time on another planet." He looked to his left. "Hey, don't be rude; it's his first time. Remember how scary it was for us on our first time?"

"Can I ask you something?"

"Whatevs." He shrugged.

I took a second to process his response before asking my question. "How do you draw your katanas? I mean, they're far longer than your arms. You shouldn't be able to draw them from your back."

"I've told you that they're enchanted, and that's what you're gonna ask me? Not 'how do they work' or 'how do they speak to you'? You're a weird little man. They're shorter when sheathed and longer when drawn."

There was a pause.

"Yo, Nine's talking to you."

"He is?"

"She, actually. You're deep into this ignoring thing, ain'tcha? Who's putting you all up to this?"

"To what?"

"The ignoring, the mind reading; I swear some of you guys are even following me."

I stared at him blankly.

"Yeah, someone put you up to this, and you don't even know it. I'll get to the bottom of it. As a member of the Tristan Corps, it's my job to sort stuff like this out."

I contemplated for a second. "Are you schizophrenic?"

"What's that?"

"Like you have difficulty interpreting reality properly. You get hallucinations, delusions; I've read about it."

He grinned at me. "Whatever makes sense to you, man. Don't worry. I'll find who's putting you all up to this."

The earthquake died down then.

"Finally," Stryx sighed. He pulled his swords out of the ground and sheathed them, and the pink circle disappeared. He started walking away. "You can come with, if you want."

"Are you talking to me?" I asked, coming to my feet.

"I am."

Having him around would probably be good for my safety. After all, if it weren't for him, I'd be dead right now. Not even the sparkling water could protect me from the fissure I almost fell into.

"I'm warning you, though," Stryx continued, "if you start reading my mind, I'm gonna have to leave you." He tapped a finger on his head. "I've got trade secrets in here."

I nodded and followed him.

Chapter 13

Stryx and I continued to wander through the desert with no end in sight. It felt like we'd been walking for at least an hour.

"Where are we going?" I asked him.

"Does it matter?" He didn't look at me.

"Yeah, kind of."

He exhaled. "We're going to a lake."

"What kind of lake?"

"Damn, man, you ask a lotta questions."

"Well, you don't necessarily answer very many."

"There's a reason for that," he mumbled.

"Have I done something to upset you?"

"I'm not the one who's upset."

I think I knew what this was about. "I'm sorry for ignoring your friends."

He exhaled. "Look, man, I know you don't mean it. None of you do. I just don't like to see my friends upset, and they've had it rough on this planet."

"Yeah, I'm sure."

"Wait!" Stryx stopped walking and wrapped his hand around the hilt of one of his sheathed swords.

"What's wrong?" I asked him.

He drew his sword and whipped it in front of my face. There was a clank of metal, and then a tiny dagger landed before my feet.

"Tri, Nine, I think you should stay with Charles," Stryx said. "I have a bad feeling about this." He drew his other sword and took a battle stance. "All right, coward, show yourself."

Three women—with varying brightly coloured skin tones and rough-looking skin textures—appeared out of nowhere, a few metres in front of us. Well, not exactly 'out of nowhere'; it was more like I hadn't noticed them until now.

The women were twirling knives and daggers between their fingers.

"You see their eyes?" Stryx whispered.

"Are you talking to me?" I wondered.

"All three of ya, really."

"Okay, what about their eyes?"

"They're red ... Exactly, the eyes of a killer."

These words awoke a memory within me. When I first came to this planet, the voice that spoke to me said that a killer would be marked with red eyes. This wasn't the first time I'd seen it either. That woman with Skylar, Trish, she had a killer's red eyes as well.

"We don't want any trouble," Stryx said to the women.

"Then we don't share the same desires," one of the women answered.

Stryx eyed them all intensely. "I'm pretty well trained, as things go. Even still, it took me a while to notice your presence. Takes a lot of skill to be able to sneak up on me. I'm guessing you practise Avertré."

"That's correct."

Stryx nodded. "Last I heard, the students of Avertré are taught to be peaceful, to respect nature and life. So why are you killing people?"

"Same reason anyone kills on this planet. Only the last survivor gets to leave this place and go home."

Stryx tightened his grip on his swords. "There's three of ya. What happens when you're the only ones left? You gonna kill each other?"

"We'll cross that bridge when it comes."

Stryx snickered slightly under his breath. "All right, I'll give ya one chance to turn around and walk."

The women laughed at his offer. "You hear that, girls? Man's giving us one chance."

"We ain't scared of you, katana boy," said another of the women.

"You should be," Stryx responded.

The women immediately stopped laughing. "All right, let's get this over with."

A dagger was launched from one of the women's hands, and it whizzed straight for us. Stryx leaped and twirled in midair, and just before he landed, he kicked the airborne dagger to the ground and threw one of his katanas at the woman. It struck right through her hand, and she fell to her knees, screaming.

The other two women dashed toward Stryx, daggers ready. Their weopons clashed against his sword. I had my sparkling water ready, just in case Stryx needed my help, but it didn't seem that he'd be needing me at all. He was holding his own quite well. Though, the women were pretty skilled also. I was surprised they had lasted this long against Stryx's sword with just their tiny knives and daggers.

In the distance, I could see the wounded woman. She was too far away to see clearly, but it looked like she wasn't bleeding at all, even though there was a katana stuck in her hand.

Stryx disarmed one of the women he was fighting with his sword and kicked her away. She landed heavily on the ground and kicked up a puff of yellow sand.

Stryx held out his hand, and as if attracted by a magnet, the sword that was stuck in the woman's hand freed itself and flew straight back to him. Then he whipped his newly obtained sword at the wounded woman closest to him at the exact moment she was coming to her feet. The sword pierced through her chest, and again, there was no blood.

Stryx continued to fight the final woman, but unfortunately, this fight wasn't going as well as the others had. The woman successfully disarmed Stryx, his sword flying out of his hand and landing in the sand. She then thrust her dagger at him repeatedly, but Stryx avoided all of her attacks and even landed a few punches. He flung his foot into the air and kicked her in the face, knocking her off balance. Then he opened his hand and called his grounded blade back to him, using it to disarm the woman and knock her to the ground. He pointed his blade at her face.

"Do it," she said. "Kill me."

Stryx grinned. "It don't work like that."

He sliced her throat, but like the others, there was no blood.

Stryx called back his other sword from the woman's chest and sheathed the both of them. "I think we're done here."

He walked away from the battlefield. "You guys coming?" I assumed he was talking to me and his friends.

I followed him, away from the defeated women.

"How did you do that?" I asked.

"There you go again, straight to the questions. Would it kill you to say thank you or something?"

"You impaled one of those women, but she's not dead, none of them even bled."

He sighed. "I already told you; my katanas aren't capable of violence. They only disperse evil. Evil is a virus, and my katanas are the cure."

"So, what, you're saying that you cured those women, as in they don't want to kill anymore?"

"Yep."

"Wow." I pondered this for a bit. "So the planets that the Tristan Corps protects, they must be pretty peaceful."

Stryx let out a small chuckle. "Yeah, you'd think that, wouldn't you?"

"Are you saying they're not?"

"Cures are temporary, lil' dude. You can always be reinfected."

That made me think of drug addictions. No matter how long you've been sober, it's always possible to have a relapse. I guess that's true for a lot of things in life, including evil, as he put it. We can all fall back into old habits without even realizing it. We think those habits help us ... even if they don't.

Stryx stopped walking. We stood in front of a small circle of grass and trees, an odd sight in the desert.

"You sure this is the place, man?" Stryx said. He didn't appear to be talking to me. "You have been wrong before. Yes, you have; don't act like you haven't. You see? Nine knows what I'm saying. All right, all right, I'll take your word for it." Stryx looked at me. "This way."

He walked into the circle of trees, and I followed him. From the inside, it was full of greenery, and in the very centre, there was a pond of sparkling water!

"No, I will not apologize," Stryx argued with his friends. "You said this was a lake; I see a pond here. Far as I'm concerned, you got lucky with this actually being a cintin water pond."

"Cintin," I cut in. "Is that what this stuff is called?"

"You're familiar with it?" Stryx looked at me.

"Yeah, it's been helping me defend myself on this planet."

"Whoa, whoa, whoa, hold on. You've been drinking this stuff?"

"Yes. Why, shouldn't I?"

"This crap causes extreme psychosis. That's why I have to get rid of it; it's too dangerous to leave alone."

"You can't!" That came out a bit louder than I wanted it to.

"I don't think you're listening, man. It's too dangerous. I've seen this water pluck at the sanity of the best of us."

"I have a bracelet; it stops the psychosis. You can't get rid of it. I need that water. I'll die without it."

"Bracelet? Send it."

"What?"

"The bracelet, send it."

I scrunched my brow. "What does that mean?"

"It means pass me the bracelet."

"Oh." I removed it from my wrist and let him see it. Under my breath, I mumbled, "Why didn't you say that in the first place?"

Stryx gazed at the leather of my bracelet. "And you're saying this thing stops the psychosis?"

"Yeah."

He scratched at it with his fingernail for a second. Then he yelled, "Shut up!" I jumped. "Sorry. Not you, them."

He pointed indiscriminately in the air. "I can't think with all the constant chatter, guys."

He went back to looking at the bracelet and then he threw it back to me. I put it back on my wrist.

"Hate to break it to you, lil' man, but that's just a leather bracelet. That ain't stopping no psychosis."

"No, but it has been," I argued. "I've been using the water to protect myself, and I feel fine."

"Everyone feels fine at first. It's a drug; it lures you in. Like it or not, that bracelet you have is just a bracelet. It won't protect you from anything. Cintin water is dangerous; I have to get rid of it."

"But I need it. I'm not like you. I can't fight. I don't have any weapons. Without the water, I'll die."

He looked at me, then at the pond of water, then he grumbled. "I don't know, what do you think, Nine? I know it doesn't look like it's affecting him and he needs it, but there are other people on this planet, and cintin water is dangerous for them. It's not something to mess around with ... All right, all right. I'm trusting your judgment. Don't make me regret it." He looked at me. "Do you have a bottle or something to keep the water in?"

"Yeah, I do."

"Okay then, here's the deal: You fill your bottle to the top with this stuff, and then that's it. I'm getting rid of it."

"But what if I need more?"

"That's the deal, man. Take it or leave it."

For a split second, I considered using the water to fight him and stop him from getting rid of it, but after seeing what he did to those women, I knew I couldn't take him in a fight. Plus, what was I going to do, kill him over the fate of some sparkling water? That would be absurd.

I retrieved the bottle from my satchel and dipped it into the pond, accepting his offer.

"Okie doke," he said. "That's the last of this water, so you'd better use it wisely."

"What do you mean 'last'?" I said while twisting the cap back onto the bottle and returning it to my satchel.

"I've been tracking these cintin water pools ever since I first found one. This is the last one in the vicinity."

Stryx drew one of his swords and dipped the blade into the water. The sword glowed with a pink sheen, and the sparkling water, the resource on this planet I have relied on the most, began to evaporate. Then there was just an empty crater in its place. It almost felt painful to watch.

Stryx sheathed his sword. "Welp, that's that."

I didn't say anything; I couldn't. I felt like I'd just watched my closest friend get murdered. My chest felt tight, my mouth was dry, and my hand lingered by my satchel, where my water was.

"Listen, man, I gotta go," Stryx said, already on his way out of the circle of trees and back into the desert. "Me and my buddies still have plenty to do. Gotta keep evil away. See ya on the flip side, dude. And if you notice the slightest slip in your sanity, throw that water away. It's not worth it, man."

I didn't answer him. I continued to stare at the emptiness of the crater long after Stryx had left. I took out my bottle of sparkling water and looked at the crater through the bottle. After letting out a heavy sigh, I, too, started on my way.

Chapter 14

My travels today had strangely brought me somewhere I don't usually go: a populated area. It almost resembled a town. There were people of a variety of creeds, all minding their own business and getting on with their lives. It seemed like these people were just making peace with the circumstances and trying to live a normal life on this planet. The area was also filled with the same cabins I keep seeing everywhere.

There was, however, one oddity. Something didn't quite belong in this environment. It was a sound, faint and yet piercing, coming from a little girl crouched over a little boy. She was crying, and the boy wasn't moving. I could only assume the worst.

Crying is a very odd thing. It's so detrimental to one's survival. It compromises the vision and makes your nose runny. But even still, there is one thing that crying is very good at doing: getting attention. No one cries unless they need something. Whether it's food, protection, or just someone to talk to, a crying person always needs something. But it seemed no one was willing to oblige. No one even wanted to check to see if the girl was okay. No one cared. Is that what this planet has done? Everyone was so focused on surviving that they'd learned not to care about people. Or maybe it has nothing to do with the circumstances; maybe they were always like that.

From all my years in school, being bullied every day, I knew what it was like to have no one care. I wasn't about to walk away from someone who needed me.

I walked past all the people who were content to mind their own business and approached the girl. As I got closer, I realized just how human the boy and girl looked. Save for their green hair and the pair of antennae on their heads, they looked like any other children on Earth.

"Are you all right?" I asked the girl, standing before her.

She slowly lifted her head, tears streaming down her face. "No-o. No-a, I don't think I am-o."

I sat down on the ground. "Who was he?"

"My-a husband, Vernon-o. We-a were married for fifty years ... and now he's gone-o. And-a the coward who killed him left only this-o." She handed me a crumpled-up piece of paper.

I unravelled it, but I couldn't read it. "What language is this?"

"Cripti-o. It-a says: *You have been saved*-o. It-a almost seems like a cruel joke-o. If-a only I'd gotten a better look at her-o."

"Her? Are you saying you saw the killer?"

"Only-a for a moment-o. She-a had a tail and tentacles for hair-o."

I pondered for a moment. "That sounds like Trish."

"Who-o?"

"Oh, just someone I know. Your description kind of sounds like her."

Without warning, the girl latched her hands onto my face. I was instantly blinded, and my eyes felt like they were melting out of their sockets. Then she let go, and I toppled over.

"Sorry-a, sorry-o," she repeated.

My sight slowly came back, and the pain gradually subsided. "What was that?"

"I'm-a sorry-o. I-a didn't mean to hurt you-o. You-a said you knew someone who looked like the killer-o. I-a had to scan your mind to see if it was her-o."

I slowly sat up. "Maybe a little warning next time."

"Sorry-o."

"Well, was it her, then?"

She smiled. "Yes-o. Thanks-a to you, I've gotten a better look at her-o. Now-a I can find her-o."

"This is a big planet. Just knowing what she looks like won't really help you find her. She could be anywhere."

"That's-a what these are for-o." She pointed to her antennae.

"What is that, some sort of radar?"

She nodded.

"How long has it been since your husband was killed?"

She looked down. "I-a don't know, probably hours-o. I've-a lost track-o."

"Well, I'm sure she can get pretty far in a few hours. You would need a fairly sizable range for your antennae to be of any use."

"I-a can see and feel everyone on this planet with my antennae-o."

"Wow, really?"

She nodded. "My-a home world is far bigger than this one-o. I'm-a surprised that the lighter gravity of this world doesn't seem to be much of an issue for me-o." She stood up. "Thank-a you-o. Now-a I can get my revenge on that husband killer-o." She grinned, and it creeped me out a little.

"Wait, you're not planning on killing her, are you?"

"Oh-a, no-o. I-a couldn't kill anyone; I don't have the guts for that-o. I-a just want to see her and give her a piece of my mind-o." She crouched down and rubbed her husband's forehead. Then she stood back up. "Would-a you ... maybe want to help me confront her-o?"

I smiled. "Sure."

"Oh-a, thank you-o." She hugged me tightly, and I clenched up, uncomfortable with the embrace. "Okay-a, let's go-o. I-a don't think she's too far away-o."

I stood and followed her lead.

"My-a name's Claudette, by the way-o. What's-a yours-o?"

"Charles."

We walked in silence for a bit, and this gave me a second to think. We were about to confront Trish, my friend, with the accusation that she had murdered Claudette's husband. It's definitely not out of the realm of possibility. She did have the red eyes of a killer, and she never believed any of this Planet-of-Shadows stuff was real. She thought it was a game, and that by killing people, she was sending them back home. Skylar and Waxton never agreed with her, though. Maybe she left their group and went off on her own, or maybe she convinced them she was right, and now they're all killing people. Maybe I'm overthinking things. Let's just see what happens when we find her.

Claudette stopped. We were deeper into the town, but it didn't really look any different from any other part of it—just lots of cabins and people.

"She's-a nearby, but I'm not sure where-o," she said. "We'll-a have to ask if anyone has seen her-o."

"I thought you said you could see everyone on the planet with your antennae."

"I-a can, but it's distorted at close range-o. Everything-a gets fuzzy-o."

"You can see everyone on the planet except for when they're right in front of you? That's lame."

"It-a is not-o!" She stuck her finger between my eyes. "Can-a you see that properly-o?"

"All right, all right." I pushed her finger away from my face. "You've made your point."

"Good-o. Now-a, we'll find her faster if we split up-o. You-a ask people that way, and I'll ask people this way-o. Yell-a if you find her-o."

"Uh, I don't think that's a good idea."

Claudette placed her hands on her hips. "Why-a not-o?"

"I'm not really comfortable just talking to people like that."

"You're-a talking to me-o."

"I mean I don't like to initiate the conversation."

"You-a initiated the conversation with me-o."

"That's different ... sort of."

She grumbled under her breath. "All-a right, fine-o. We'll-a ask people together-o. But-a you're kind of odd, you know that-o?"

"Odd?"

"Well-a, not exactly 'odd'-o. I-a don't know how I would describe you-o. I'm-a sure it will come to me-o."

We walked around and asked passersby if they had seen anyone who looked like Trish, and after we had asked a sizable amount of people, one of them proved to be helpful.

"Yeah, she sounds familiar," a man said. "I think I saw someone like that go into that cabin up ahead."

"Great-a, let's go-o." Claudette headed straight for the cabin.

I thanked the man for his help and followed her.

We stood at the door of the cabin, hesitating.

Claudette took a few deep breaths. "I-a can do this-o. I-a can do this-o." She squeezed my hand.

"What are you doing?" I wondered, feeling a little uncomfortable.

She pulled her hand away. "Nothing-o. I'm-a just … a little bit … scared-o."

I smiled. "It'll be fine. We're just going to talk to her and give her a piece of your mind, right?"

"Right-o. Just-a … giving her a piece of my mind-o."

I got my bottle of sparkling water from my satchel and took a sip.

"Is-a that water-o?"

"Yeah."

"You're-a thirsty, at a time like this-o?"

I shook my head. "No, it's not for thirst."

"Then-a why did you drink it-o?"

Good question. I didn't even think; I just drank some. "It's, um … insurance," I told her, putting the bottle back in my satchel. "Just in case this doesn't go as planned."

She looked away and took a deep breath. Her hand stretched out toward the door; it wouldn't stop shaking. She looked at me, and I nodded. She smiled, and together, we opened the door.

The inside of the cabin was set up like a restaurant, in the sense that there were tables and chairs everywhere. But unlike a restaurant, this cabin wasn't crowded with people. There was only one. Trish sat at a table on the far end of the cabin, drinking from a glass and twirling her tentacle hair with her finger.

"Charles!" she called. "How are you? I have not seen you in some time."

"You-a shut your mouth, husband killer-o," Claudette snapped.

"What?" Trish was taken aback by Claudette's aggression.

She stomped over to Trish. I followed her lead, albeit in a more reserved manner. We both sat at Trish's table.

"Don't-a act like you don't know what I'm talking about-o." She pointed her finger at Trish.

Trish just stared blankly at Claudette. "I cannot even understand what you are saying."

"You-a killed my husband-o!"

Trish flashed her red-eyed gaze to me and shrugged.

"She's accusing you of killing her husband," I clarified.

"How can you understand her?"

"It's not that hard. She's just adding an A at the beginning of her sentence and an O at the end. I've heard enough different dialects on this planet to be used to it."

"I cannot hear any of that. She might as well be speaking a different language."

"Stop-a changing the subject-o!" Claudette screamed.

Trish looked at me again. "Translation?"

"She's still talking about you killing her husband."

"Oh." She rolled her eyes.

There was a silence.

"Did you?" I asked.

"Did I what?"

"Kill her husband."

"Oh, right. I do not remember. Probably."

"Probably?" I repeated, a little shocked.

"I-a knew it-o! She-a admitted it-o!" Claudette pointed and yelled at Trish, almost jumping out of her seat.

"Trish, what do you mean by 'probably'?" I asked, trying to keep things calm.

"Charles, come on. Are you not tired of this?"

"Tired of what?"

"This game. Do you not want to go home?"

"Trish, this isn't a game."

"Of course it is, Charles. We are all trapped in a sadistic game, and the fastest way to escape is to lose it. I am speeding up the process. I am saving lives."

"Trish, you can't just kill people."

"Sure I can. It is very easy. Nobody suspects that I will kill them."

"You have a killer's red eyes; what do you mean nobody suspects you'll kill them?"

She pulled an object from her tentacle hair that I immediately recognized as sunglasses. "I wear this over my eyes. I do not know what it is, but it makes everything look darker, and it hides my eyes from people." She stuck the sunglasses back in her hair. "I found it in a cabin somewhere."

I didn't think I was going to be able to convince her that she could be wrong about any of this. I had to try a different approach. "Okay, let's assume for a second that you're right about all this—"

"I am right."

"Even if you are right," I continued. "Even if people do return home after they die, think about the people who cared about those you've killed." I looked to Claudette, who was trying very hard to hold back tears.

Trish looked at her, too. "Look, there is no reason to be upset. Your husband is back where she came from. I am sure she is fine."

"*He*-o! My-a husband is a *he*-o," Claudette simmered.

Trish looked to me for a translation.

"She says her husband is a *he*," I explained.

Trish made a weird face. "Ew, gross! You married a man? How can you even live like that? I think I would absolutely die of disgust if I had to be with a man."

"Don't-a you dare talk about my Vernon like that-o! You-a are a husband killer-o! You-a are a dirty, dirty, husband killer-o!"

"Okay, I heard *dirty*, so I take it you are still not happy with me. Look, antenna lady, you clearly miss your ... husband." Trish stuck out her yellow tongue like she was going to vomit. "I promise you, she ... *he* is back home, probably waiting for you. I can take you to him if you want, and you two can be together again."

"Wait a minute," I interrupted. "You're not talking about killing Claudette, are you?"

"Do not make it sound so violent, Charles. It will be quick; promise." Trish lifted her hand. I instinctively pushed Claudette out of her chair as Trish shot a sharp, green needle from her finger. The needle pinned itself into the back of the chair.

"Trish, are you insane?" I yelled.

She slammed her hands down and lifted herself up, flipping over onto the table in a crouching position. She looked a lot like a contortionist.

She shot a few more needles at the grounded Claudette, but I lifted an empty chair and used it to block them.

"Trish, stop," I said. "She doesn't want this. This isn't a game."

She prepared to shoot even more needles, but I threw the chair at her, temporarily stunning her.

It was a good thing I drank the sparkling water before I came in here, but I wasn't sure how much longer it would last, so I had to handle this quickly.

I helped Claudette off the floor.

"This-a isn't going well at all-o," she whimpered.

"Don't worry," I reassured. "We'll be okay."

I led her closer to the door, but before we got too far, Trish recovered. She raised her hand and shot more needles at us. Where were they even coming from? Were they organic needles or is she storing them somewhere? I kicked over one of the nearby tables, grabbed Claudette's hand, and pulled her behind my frantically constructed cover. The tips of Trish's needles could be seen on our side of the table, as they stuck right through the wood.

"To-a be honest, I didn't think this is how this would go-o," Claudette confessed.

"Well, in hindsight, she did kill your husband. How did you think this was going to go? Did you really think she would be willing to just talk?"

"I-a don't know-o. I-a thought maybe I would yell at her for an hour and then leave-o."

"Seriously?"

"I-a am a mourning widow now; I'm not thinking straight-o."

Trish knocked our table away with a kick. Claudette cowered behind me, and I stood to my full height to better protect her.

"Move, Charles," Trish demanded.

"Come on, Trish, stop this. Someone's going to get hurt."

"That is kind of the idea."

"Why are you doing this? What happened to helping people with Waxton and Skylar?"

"I am tired of helping people. I want to go home, Charles. Do you not want to go home?"

"Of course I do, but this is not the way. There's someone keeping us here. We have to find and stop them; that's the only way any of us are getting out of here."

"Do you understand the logistics of that? To kidnap one hundred people from fifty planets and trap us all here, to construct this entire planet? It is ridiculous, Charles. This is a game, and I am helping people end it. Now move."

She extended needles halfway out of her fingertips and swiped at me. I did a decent job of avoiding her attacks, but she still managed to hit me a few times. The water was definitely wearing off.

Her attacks were backing me up against a wall. I ducked out of the way, and she accidentally hit her hand against it.

"Ah!" she said, shaking the pain out of her hand.

Then a chair flew through the air and shattered over Trish's head. The force of the impact smacked her into the wall, and she slowly slid to the ground, motionless.

I looked to see where the chair had come from. I wasn't sure what I was expecting, but what I saw was a very startled Claudette. In all the commotion, I hadn't even realized that she'd moved from behind me.

She cupped her hands over her mouth. "What-a did I just do-o?"

"You ... how did you lift that chair? No, that's not what I want to ask. I—"

"Do-a you think she's dead-o?" Claudette's eyes were darting across the floor.

I went to her side. "Try to calm down. This isn't your fault."

"No-a, it is-o. I-a am a murderer-o."

"She was trying to kill you; you acted in self-defence. You're not a murderer."

As if in response to what I said, Trish began to move.

"Oh, what happened?" she groaned, staggering to her feet.

"Trish, are you okay?" I asked.

"Who is Trish?" She pulled one of the tentacles on her head in front of her eyes. She seemed almost confused by it.

"*You're* Trish," I reminded her.

"I am?"

Claudette repeatedly tapped my arm and whispered, "I-a think she has amnesia-o."

There was a clank as Trish's sunglasses fell to the ground. "Whoa, look what fell out of my head," she said. "What is that?"

She looked up and stumbled over to me. "Do I know you?"

I looked at Trish, and then at Claudette cowering behind me again. "Uh ... no. No, we don't know each other."

I gestured for Claudette to follow me, and we both exited the cabin without another word.

"Why-a did you lie to her-o?" she asked me.

I sighed. "Even when I first met Trish, she always thought all this was just a game. I can't convince her otherwise, so maybe it's best for everyone if we just let her forget about it all."

"I-a guess so-o. I-a feel kind of bad-o. This-a is all my fault-o."

"No it's not. It's this planet, the circumstances. It makes us all show our true colours, and it makes us all do what we have to do to survive. That's all you did, survive."

She looked up at me. "Still-a, I hope she's okay-o. She-a may be a husband killer, but I didn't want it to go like this-o. I-a just wanted to yell at her for a bit-o."

Claudette and I walked through the busy town, becoming part of the mass of people with untold stories. This was the first time I'd noticed that no one was really talking to each other. We were all silent ... together, alone.

I got my bottle of sparkling water out from my satchel and stared at my face reflected in it. There were only two-thirds of it left. Because of Stryx. He got rid of it. He took it. And I just drank it. Sure, I ended up needing it, but I didn't know that when I drank it. What do I do when there's none left? (*Charles.*) (*Charles.*)

"Charles-o?" Claudette's voice ripped me from my thoughts.

"Huh? Did you say something?" I put my bottle back after taking a quick sip.

"I-a said thank you-o."

"Oh, uh, you're welcome."

She smiled. "You-a know, when all of this started, we were told that only the last survivor could go home-o.

For-a the longest time, I couldn't imagine life without my Vernon, and I knew he wouldn't have been able to imagine life without me-o. But-a now he's gone, I don't think I even want to go home anymore-o."

"What do you mean?"

"I-a just mean that I'm content, you know-o? I-a don't care if I get to go home; it won't be the same-o. Whatever-a happens tomorrow, I'll be okay with it-o. I-a think … you should be the one to go home-o."

"Me?"

"Yeah-o. I-a was a stranger to you, but you helped me anyway-o. You-a protected me; you cared about me-o. You're-a one of the kindest people I've ever met, and I don't want you to die-o. I-a want you to be the one who lives on to see a life after the Planet of Shadows-o."

I thought about how little sparkling water I had left. "Unfortunately, I don't think that's very likely."

She giggled. "I-a think I've found the perfect word to describe you-o. You-a are robotic-o."

"Robotic?" That word struck a chord with me. Claudette wasn't the first person to call me that; I've heard it a few times in my life. "Why do you think I'm robotic?"

"Because-a you're different-o. You-a don't fully understand the people around you, but you try to fit in anyway, even if you can't-o. You're-a just like a robot— similar to everyone else but not quite like everyone else-o."

My face fell.

"I-a don't mean that as a bad thing-o," she assured me. "You're-a different, and I think that's a good thing-o. I-a mean, no one else came to help me-o. I-a was crying over my husband's body for hours, and no one cared-o. But-a you did-o." She wrapped her arms around my waist and hugged me tightly. "Thank-a you-o."

And for the first time, a hug didn't make me feel entirely uncomfortable.

Chapter 15

Rain poured down the long tree leaves of the dense forest I found myself in. I was alone. Claudette had offered for us to travel together, but I declined. I don't really know why.

Raindrops plummeted on my forehead. Even though the trees provided partial shelter from the rain, that didn't stop me from getting soaked.

I continued through the forest, my hand practically glued to my forehead with how often I had to wipe the rain off it. I had no idea where I was going, but I never really do, do I?

Soon, after a bit more walking, I reached some sort of clearing—no trees in sight but plenty of grass. There was a cabin there, just like all the others. I ran to it, thinking only of the shelter it would provide.

Letting myself in, I closed the door and shook the rain out of my hair like a wet dog. There didn't seem to be anyone here. The rain continued to pelt the roof of the cabin, but thankfully, I could no longer feel it.

I looked around. There was nothing remarkable about the furnishing here. There was a small lamp on the floor next to a window on the left, and a sofa next to another window on the right. Near the back of the cabin was a long table cluttered with beakers and test tubes and other cylindrical containers, all filled with strangely coloured liquids. At the end of this long table sat a desktop computer with a keyboard and mouse plugged into it.

I ran to it. I hadn't seen a computer in such a long time. Examining the keyboard, I realized it was in English. Maybe that meant the computer was from Earth. I'd always felt comfortable with computers. They have uniform, unchanging rules that I could easily understand. It felt familiar on a planet where nothing was familiar.

I pressed what I assumed was the power button and frowned. When the computer booted up, the monitor was filled with symbols I couldn't understand. I guess the computer was alien but the keyboard wasn't.

Then a sound echoed throughout the cabin, like someone had knocked something over. I looked, but nothing had fallen. The only thing was that the shadow of the lamp seemed bigger somehow. It stretched across the room and to the other end of the cabin. The sun must have changed position outside.

I went back to fiddling with the computer.

"I wonder," I said to myself. "If I can find some sort of word processor on this thing, maybe I can use that to help me translate the writing on the screen."

I clicked on an icon that sort of resembled paper with writing on it. Once it loaded, the screen turned white, and there was a blinking cursor there. Maybe this computer was from Earth; it worked a lot like the computers I was used to. Maybe it was just set to a language I didn't recognize.

I typed the letter A, and the corresponding symbol showed up on the screen. I planned to use this method to make a decryption key of sorts. I continued the process for a bit until I was interrupted by the same noise I'd heard before. I darted my eyes across the room, but still, nothing was out of place … except that same lamp shadow, or rather, lack thereof. It was gone! Now I knew something was wrong.

I walked over to the lamp and stared at it. I was wrong. There was a shadow, but it was tiny, as if it were a shadow for a lamp five times smaller. The position of the sun couldn't do that.

Before I had any time to ponder this, the door slammed open, and a man with a scorpion tail ran in and shut the door back. He used his tail to wipe rain out of his spiky, green hair. In his hand was a brown bag with something inside, though I couldn't see what.

"Who are you?" he asked, startled. "Why are you in my house?"

I froze, trying not to seem threatening in any way. "Sorry, I didn't know anyone lived here," I explained. "I was just trying to get out of the rain."

"Oh, okay, then. But I've got my eye on you." He didn't seem very upset at my intrusion.

He walked over to the long table and rearranged the beakers and test tubes, making room for his bag. He emptied out its contents—a variety of colourful berries. Using his tail, he began chopping them up into little pieces.

I glanced over at the lamp's shadow again. It was back to its regular size. "Um, do the shadows here usually change size so quickly?" I asked the man, hoping this was a normal occurrence.

"Change size?" He looked at me.

"Yeah, this lamp's shadow has been acting strangely. It keeps changing size."

The man rushed over to the lamp and stared at the shadow. He stuck his finger out to touch it, and the shadow moved away from him before he even made contact.

"Oh no," he said.

"What's wrong?"

He rushed back over to the long table. "They can't come now; I'm not ready. I haven't prepared the thing."

"Who's coming?"

"I don't know what they are, some kind of pitch-black, canine-looking things. I call them shadow-beasts. They emit a sort of magnetic pulse that affects the shadows; makes them do weird things. I've been keeping them at bay with an EMP I made."

"And that keeps them away?"

"Yeah. It counteracts their own magnetic pulse and repels them. But the last time they were here, I didn't act fast enough, and they destroyed it. I've been gradually trying to gather resources to repair it, but it's not done yet." The man fished out a box from underneath the long table. I hadn't even noticed it before. He got out some parts from it, assumedly for the EMP.

"Why do the shadow-beasts come here?" I wondered.

"I don't know. But they destroy things when they're here." He got to work putting various pieces together and muttered, "I don't have enough time."

"How much time do you need?"

"I don't know, maybe ten minutes. But judging by the lamp's shadow, the shadow-beasts will be here in two."

I retrieved my bottle of sparkling water from my satchel. There was a little over half of it left. I couldn't; it was too valuable. I had to preserve it. I had to ...

"What if I hold the shadow-beasts off while you repair the EMP?" I said.

"They're tough. How do you plan to hold them off?"

"With this." I pointed at my bottle.

"What's that?"

"It's a long story. I'll tell you when we're finished."

And then the room darkened. The shadows had grown very large.

"I hope you know what you're doing," the man said, "because they're here."

From the enlarged shadows emerged pitch-black, canid creatures, just like the man had described. They varied in size, some as large as bears, others as small as mice. All of them growled. I sipped my water and got to work.

The beasts lunged for me, and I pushed them back. It wasn't the most graceful or interesting fight, but it got the job done. As long as they didn't interrupt the EMP's reconstruction.

But then the water began to wear off. Odd, it usually lasts longer than that. One of the shadow-beasts took advantage of this and quickly knocked me down, standing over me. I jammed my arm into its neck to keep it from biting me, and with strength conjured up from adrenalin alone, I pushed the beast away.

"They're getting closer," said the man.

I got up and pushed away the beast closest to him. It ran and leaped into a shadow as if it were a deep pool of water. My muscles were aching. The water had definitely worn off; I was really starting to feel this fight. I sipped some more of it and continued on.

The shadow-beasts weren't slowing down. The ones I'd pushed back ran away into the shadows, but they were soon replaced with more. These things were never-ending, but I could only last as long as the water could.

"How much longer?" I asked.

"Five minutes ... hopefully." The man worked vigorously.

A shadow-beast the size of a bear lunged at me. I pushed it away, but it just came straight back. This one didn't want to give up, and there were still smaller ones coming. Keeping them at bay was easy for a time, but then the water began to wear off again. Why was this happening? Why was it wearing off so quickly?

One of the beasts tackled me to the ground. I pushed it aside, but more soon followed. They pinned me down; I couldn't get to my water. I was trapped.

"I hope you're almost done," I said. "I don't think I can hold them off much longer."

"Almost."

I jerked my body enough to make the shadow-beasts lose their balance, and with my arm, I held back the one closest to me. Its face was so close to mine that I couldn't see it properly without crossing my eyes.

"I could really use that EMP right now," I called.

"One second."

"I don't have one second."

"Now!"

There was a sort of vibrating sound, and then the shadow-beasts disappeared like smoke.

I stood up. The man stood next to his reconstructed EMP, breathing heavily.

"Did it," he gasped.

"You did."

"Thank you for your help, Mister ..."

"McCoy. But just call me Charles."

"Okay, cool. I'm Liz."

I scratched my head. "Sorry, I thought you were a man all this time."

"I am."

"But isn't Liz a girl's name?"

"Not that I know of."

He started tampering with his EMP, probably trying to turn it off. Then he walked over to the computer.

"Why is the word processor open?" he wondered.

"Oh, sorry. I was using it to decrypt the writing on the screen."

"But to do that you'd need ... Wait, can you read the language on the keyboard?"

"Yeah."

"Oh, my sticks and bricks, you can help me decipher it. And, for that matter, you can help defend me when the shadow-beasts come back. You have to stay with me. Please. I'll share my food with you, and this cabin is just as much yours as it is mine."

I considered the offer. Maybe I should (*stay*). Maybe (*stay*)ing could be a good thing. I'll watch his back, and he'll watch mine. We can help each other out, teach each other stuff.

I retrieved my bottle of sparkling water. I wanted to (*stay*), but I barely had a quarter of the bottle left. I won't be able to defend myself when it's gone.

"I want to stay, but without my sparkling water, I'm not very well equipped to defend against anything here." I showed him how much was left.

He walked over and examined the water. "What's it do?"

"It makes me faster, stronger."

"Like a drug or a performance enhancer?"

"I guess so."

"Well, have you ever thought about concentrating it?"

"You mean like boiling it down?"

"To make more, yeah. We'll need regular water to mix the concentrated solution into, but it should work."

I stared at my nearly empty bottle. "What if it doesn't work? I don't know what this stuff is made of; what if we boil it down and it just evaporates? Then I won't have any left."

"You're going to run out of it soon anyway. At least this way, there's a decent chance we can make it last longer." Liz motioned his head toward the beakers and containers on the long table. "There're plenty of things over there we can use to concentrate the water. Plus, if we make enough of it, we can both drink it, and then we'd both be able to defend against the shadow-beasts."

"No!" I said, a little louder than I wanted to.

"No? Why not?"

I showed him my bracelet. "The water causes extreme psychosis unless you're wearing this bracelet."

Liz eyed the leather around my wrist. "Are you sure? I mean, have you ever tested it?"

"No, and I don't plan to. I've heard the same story from two people now, and I don't want to find out if they're right."

"Fair enough. So is that a *yes*, then? Will you (*stay*)?"

(*Stay.*)

(*Stay.*)

"Can you hear that?"

"Hear what?" Liz questioned.

"I don't know. I thought I ..." I shook my head. "Never mind. I'll stay."

"You will?"

"Yeah."

"Yes! We are going to have so much fun together." He walked over to the long table where he'd left his berries and resumed chopping them up with his tail. "Do you want some of these?"

When he said this, my stomach rumbled. "Yeah, sure. Sounds good."

Chapter 16

Over the next few days, Liz and I were able to successfully concentrate the sparkling water, and we spent time mixing it with regular water to make more and teaching each other different skills. He's been teaching me how to cook with the berries on this planet (though it didn't always go so well), and I've been teaching him how to read English, which was a lot easier than it could have been due to the fact that all speech was fully translated on this planet. Plus, Liz seemed to have the same grammatical practices as I did, aside from the odd expression here and there.

Today, we were walking through the forest on a sunny day looking for more regular water to mix with the concentrated sparkling water. We had already made enough to refill my bottle and to have a few reserve bottles, but we needed more water to make enough to last us a while. I carried a bucket—which I got from the cabin—to store the water in. Liz would have brought a bucket, too, but he didn't like to use his hands much. He said he had weak wrists. So I did most of the handy work.

"Do you know where we'll find water?" I asked him.

"There used to be a pond farther down."

"Right, we walked by it yesterday. It's dried up, though."

"Yeah. But I'm thinking, if we go there anyway, it might lead us to another source of water."

"Guess that's as good a plan as any." I nodded.

The leafy trees of the forest were rife with alien sounds—buzzing, whistling, scraping, and clicking.

"Do you have these things on Earth?" Liz asked.

"What, the trees?"

"Yeah, these tall things." He pointed around at them.

"There're tons of them on Earth. Aren't there any trees on Cal-So?"

"No, we don't have anything like that."

"Not even flowers?" I wondered.

"I don't know what those are."

"So your planet doesn't have any plant life at all?"

"I guess not." Liz shrugged.

"But then, what do you breathe?"

"Air." He drew the word out, staring at me with squinted eyes.

"But plants make the air."

"They do?"

"They take in carbon dioxide and turn it into oxygen, which makes up most of the air we breathe."

"You mean you just get air from nature, like, for free?"

"Yeah. What, you don't?"

"On Cal-So, there's a machine in the centre of the planet that makes the air and feeds it into everyone's homes, as long as we pay the air bill."

I chuckled. "I'm sure if the people on my planet could figure out how to make money off of air consumption, they would."

"Makes me wonder, though, how do the people who don't breathe oxygen breathe on this planet?"

I pondered this. "Maybe everyone here breathes oxygen. It wouldn't be a stretch. After all, everyone here is humanoid. Maybe it was imperative to whoever's running this planet that everyone breathes the same thing."

Liz nodded. "Sense bent. Do you ever wonder about the person who brought us all here?"

I sighed. "All the time."

"In the beginning, he said something about collecting data, didn't he? What do you think the data's for?"

"I think he said it was for an experiment."

"What kind of experiment would warrant the abduction of one hundred people and the creation of an entirely new planet? How would you even go about creating a new planet?"

I shrugged. "With some pretty advanced science, I suppose."

We walked for a bit longer, engaging in slightly less thoughtful conversation until we arrived at the dried-up pond that Liz had spoken of.

"Well," I said, "here's the dried-up pond. Where to now?"

Liz looked around. "Uh ... maybe there's water in that cave over there." He pointed to a secluded, rocky cavern in the distance.

I shrugged. "Let's go find out."

We walked a little farther until we reached the cave entrance, then we went in.

The walls inside were coated with blue rocks that illuminated the cave, and the roof near the cave entrance had water dripping down from it.

"There must be water somewhere in this cave." I pointed to the droplets.

Liz nodded, and then he plunged his scorpion tail into the stone ground.

"What are you doing?" I asked.

"So we don't get lost, I'll walk with my tail in the ground and etch a trail for us to follow back here."

"Good thinking." I smiled.

We proceeded and walked straight until we eventually arrived at a more open part of the cave. By "open" I mean like the size of Liz's and my cabin, but it definitely wasn't as full. Quite the opposite really, it was empty, and there were no water droplets here. There were only two paths, the one we just came from, and an unexplored one directly ahead.

We continued to walk forward, down the unexplored path. We were walking for a little while when something strange happened. We arrived at another open part of the cave, very similar to the last one, or rather, exactly the same. On the ground, we could see the trail Liz was making with his tail going down the path we just came from, as if we'd turned around.

"Uh ... how did we get back here?" Liz asked.

"Maybe we got turned around and didn't notice?" This was more of a question than an answer.

"How could we not notice turning around?"

"Maybe the cave loops back on itself, and the turn wasn't sharp enough to notice."

Puzzled, we decided to go back down the path to see if we could detect the turn.

Again, we arrived at the same place. There were two tail markings now, signifying that we'd travelled the same path twice.

"What is going on here?" Liz said. "I'm sure we were going completely straight."

"Me too."

"So how did we get back here?"

I put my hand over my mouth and thought about the situation. "Maybe ... maybe the cave is moving."

He looked at me. "Do caves move on Earth?"

"Not particularly, no."

"Then why would you think the cave is moving?"

"I don't know. Do you have a better explanation?"

He thought for a second. "Portals?"

"Do you have a lot of portals on Cal-So?"

"Not … particularly, no."

I sighed. "Let's head back to the entrance."

"Why would we do that?"

"Because if going forward takes us backward, then maybe going backward will take us forward."

Liz looked in the direction of the cave entrance. "But if you're right about that, how do we get out of this cave?"

"I suppose we'll cross that bridge when we come to it. Let's go."

We proceeded back to the entrance. Liz's tail was still plunged into the ground, just in case the trail could be of use to us later on.

Sure enough, my theory was correct. We were in another similarly open room, but the ground had no tail markings, so we hadn't been here yet.

"Great," Liz complained. "The path to the entrance leads here now, so we're trapped."

"Let's just find what we came for," I suggested, trying to calm him down.

In this new area, there were another two paths, the one we came from, and a new one.

This process of deciding whether to go forward or backward to unlock a new part of the cave went on for a while, until we finally arrived at a part of the cave with a small pond of water in the centre.

"Finally," said Liz. "This has got to be the most infuriating place I've ever had to navigate."

I approached the pond and filled my bucket with water.

"All right," I said. "We've got what we came for. Now, how do we get back?"

Liz didn't weigh in. He was preoccupied with something on the walls. Not the luminous blue rocks, but something scribbled on them.

"What is that?" I questioned.

"I don't know. It kind of looks like writing."

Liz ran over to the wall, and I followed his lead.

"It is writing," I said, once I was close enough to get a better look at it. "Weird how it's in English."

"No it's not; it's written in So-Lian," Liz pointed out.

I looked closer, but I couldn't agree. It was definitely English.

"Is it possible that the same writing appears differently depending on who's reading it?" I wondered.

"Maybe. I've never heard of anything like that, though."

The writing read as follows:

You have entered my cave
And found the prize you seek.
Don't try to go back
Lest you become weary and weak.
If you mean to leave
Then do beware,
For without a good memory

You'll be met with despair.
The exit is far
Yet ever so near.
Call to me
When the answer is clear.
If you are right,
And I deem it fair,
Rest assured,
I shall take you there.

Xania

"Oh, I hate riddles," Liz said.

I considered the riddle. "Why would we need a good memory?"

"Probably because it wants us to remember the path we took to get here." Liz slapped the palm of his hand to his forehead.

"No, I don't think that's it. The path keeps changing; it would be impossible to track where we were going, let alone recall it. There's got to be something else we're meant to remember."

"I can't believe this," Liz spiralled.

"It'll be fine. It's just a riddle. We just have to think about it."

"But what if we can't solve it? We've finally found the water we were looking for, and now we're trapped."

"Wait a minute." What he said jogged something in my memory. "... Water."

"What?"

"Water. There were water droplets at the entrance of the cave."

"So?"

"So they were *only* at the entrance, nowhere else."

"And?"

"Water droplets don't just appear out of nowhere," I explained. "What if the droplets are what we're meant to remember? If there were water droplets falling from the ceiling at the cave entrance, they had to have had a source. And the only place we've seen water in this whole cave is this pond right here. I bet the entrance is directly below us."

Liz raised a brow. "Well, that doesn't help. You don't expect us to tunnel down to the entrance, do you?"

"Of course not. We'll just do what the riddle says: call it when the answer is clear."

"How do we do that?"

I shrugged. "By name, I guess."

I looked at the writing again, noticing that it was signed "Xania".

I shrugged and gave it a try. "Xania, the entrance is directly below us."

Almost immediately after I said this, laughter began to echo throughout, sounding like the laughter of a young girl. And then, Liz and I found ourselves back at the entrance, bucket of water in hand.

We both looked around with perplexed expressions. We were definitely back at the entrance, but Liz's trail was gone.

"Let's leave before we get lost again," said Liz.

I nodded, and we both started for the exit. But before we left, the voice of a little girl said, "Thanks for playing with me."

I looked at Liz. "Did you hear that?"

"Yeah. But do you want to just pretend we didn't and go home?"

"Yeah."

***

When we made it back to the cabin, it was nighttime. We put the bucket of water in the corner and went about our usual business.

I looked at my bottle of sparkling water. Today was one of the few days I didn't need it. It's weird that I find that strange. There was a time when I'd never heard of this stuff, and now, I couldn't imagine not needing it. It made me feel uneasy.

I watched the water twinkle in the bottle. Then I unscrewed the cap and drank from it, and I wasn't sure why.

I screwed the cap back on and stared fondly at the collection of sparkling water Liz and I had been able to produce. We had four containers of it lined up on the long table ... But that wasn't right. I'm sure there were five containers when we left.

"Hey, Liz," I called.

"Yeah?" He looked up from the computer.

"Weren't there five containers of sparkling water before?"

"Uh, no, I don't think so."

"Are you sure?"

Liz took longer to answer this time. "Oh, you know, I think I used the fifth one for testing, to see how close it was to the original."

"When did you do that? There were five containers here when we left."

"Yeah, but only four were full. I just put away the empty one, just now."

I kept staring at him.

"Come on, Charles, don't be so paranoid. I swear, I just used it for testing. No one stole it or anything."

He was probably right. I've felt like this before, when Stryx got rid of the sparkling water. I get protective, like I'd be willing to kill someone over it. I need to relax. It isn't that serious. We have plenty of sparkling water.

Liz retrieved some berries from a bag, the same bag of berries he had before. They seem to last quite a while.

"How about dinner?" he said. "I'll show you a new recipe, a really famous delicacy on Cal-So—well, as close as we can get with the ingredients we have."

I joined him, and together, we cooked the night away.

Chapter 17

My eyes cracked open, waking from a nightmare I could no longer remember. I sat up on the sofa and held my head in my hands. I had a bit of a headache. Since there were no beds in the cabin, Liz and I always just slept on the sofa. But Liz wasn't sleeping next to me as usual; he was standing in the middle of the room, and he had a strange grin on his face.

"You're up early," he said.

"Bad dream."

"Yeah, I bet." He looked at me, and his grin disappeared. "You feeling okay?"

"Yeah, just a little headache. What are you doing up? Don't you usually sleep longer than I do?"

"No, I sleep about the same as you."

Then I noticed where he was standing—right between me and the table where we kept our sparkling water.

I stood. "Liz, move."

"What?"

"Move away from the table."

He hesitated. "I don't think ..."

"I said move!"

"Okay, okay, relax. Just calm down. I just don't think you're ready."

I stormed over, and he stepped aside. And there it was. Someone (*stole*) our sparkling water. There were only two containers left of it.

"Liz, what happened?"

He hesitated. Why was he hesitating? Did he (*steal it*)? He wouldn't. (*He would.*) How could he? I thought he was my friend. (*He lied.*)

"You stole it," I accused him. "You took the water for yourself."

"Charles, I swear, I didn't."

"Yes, you did. You must have drunk it. You wanted to be as strong as I am. You want to be strong enough to get rid of me and take the water for yourself."

"Charles, stop. I didn't take anything. Think about it. I don't have a bracelet like you. If I drank the sparkling water, wouldn't I go insane or something? Isn't that what Stryx told you?"

I took a breath. He was right. What was I doing?

"But if you didn't drink it," I said, "then where is the rest of the sparkling water? We made enough to fill ten containers the other day. There're only two here."

He was squirming. He wasn't telling me everything. He was (*hiding*) something from me.

"Liz, what aren't you telling me?" I stepped toward him, and he stepped back.

"Charles, don't worry about it. We can make more. We'll be fine."

(*He's lying.*) "Tell me what happened to it."

"It doesn't matter."

"Now!"

"You drank it!"

I paused. "No, I didn't."

"You wake up in the middle of the night and down the water. I've seen you do it."

(*He's lying.*) "That doesn't make any sense. Stop lying."

"I'm not lying. Remember what Stryx said. If I drank it, I'd be hallucinating, under full psychosis. But I'm fine. I didn't drink the water."

He did seem fine. He didn't seem like he was lying, but ... "How do you know about Stryx?"

"You told me about him," he answered simply.

"But I never told you his name."

Then his face fell, and he said calmly, "I thought you knew."

"Knew? Knew what?"

"That I'm not really here."

"What are you talking about?"

He tapped a finger on his head. "I'm up here, in your head."

Then it hit me. The whole time I'd been with Liz, he hadn't actually done anything. He hadn't interacted with the world in any way. I did all the work. I cooked, I made the sparkling water, I carried the water out of the cave with the bucket. He said it was because he had weak wrists, but could it be that he never really existed in the first place? No, wait. He made the EMP to stop those shadow-beasts. But what if I imagined them as well?

"You're not real," I mumbled, backing away from Liz.

"No, no, of course I'm real. Everything we've been through together, we're friends, Charles, aren't we? Just because I'm in your head, doesn't mean I'm not real."

Stryx was right. My bracelet isn't magic; it's just a bracelet. It hasn't been protecting me at all. The sparkling water has been slowly infecting me from the very start.

"Charles?" Liz stepped closer.

"Stay away from me!"

I backed away, but I was so flustered that I wasn't watching where I was going. I backed into the long table and knocked it hard. The force of the impact knocked one of the containers of sparkling water over, and it hit the lamp on the other end of the room. The bulb broke and mixed with the sparkling water. And then it caught fire. I thought I could hear it screaming. The water needed me. It was dying.

The fire was growing rapidly; it was going to explode. But I didn't care. It was dying. My hope was dying. And it was his fault. (*Kill.*) It was Liz's fault. (*Kill.*)

I whipped my gaze toward Liz and charged for him. The fire behind me continued to grow, but I was too focused on Liz to care. I could feel the sparkling water guiding my hand, speaking to me. (*Kill him. Kill him so we can be together. We need each other. Kill him.*)

I wailed on him with everything I had, as if all the time we'd spent together these past days meant nothing. They did mean nothing. He wasn't even real. He didn't exist. He was just the part of my mind that was dumb enough to fight—the part of me that didn't understand how much I needed the sparkling water.

(*Kill.*)

Kill.

Kill.

And then the fire roared and exploded.

***

I awoke, sprawled on the ground outside. The warmth from the destroyed, flaming cabin caressed my face. I must have passed out. I came to my feet, thinking about how lucky I was to be alive ... that, or it was the water's doing. If I really did drink it, it was probably still in my system. But it wouldn't be for long.

After that thought, I charged into the debris of the cabin, looking for any trace of sparkling water that may have survived. Never mind that the debris was hot, and I was burning my hands looking for sparkling water. Pain was irrelevant; the water was going to wear off, and I needed more.

Then, in the corner of my eye, I saw its glimmer. The bottle I kept in my satchel. It must have fallen out.

It was full.

It survived.

I ran to it and picked it up. It was just the one bottle, but it was all I needed.

It spoke to me. *"You came back for me, Charles."*

"Of course I did. I need you."

"Then drink me, bond with me. I can protect you."

I brought the bottle to my lips, but I didn't drink. My eyes were fixated on my wrist. The bracelet. The simple, non-magical, leather bracelet.

My perception had changed. Whether it was because I was strong enough to resist or because the effects of the water were wearing off, I didn't know. But I couldn't drink, not when I was this close to being free. I've been drinking the sparkling water for almost as long as I've been on this planet, even when I didn't need it. Stryx was right. He never should have let me keep it. But he still helped me. He got rid of it everywhere else. The bottle in my hands is the last of it. The supply I made has all burned and evaporated. This is it. All I have to do is leave the bottle here and walk away. Then I'll be free.

"What are you waiting for?" the voice said. *"Drink me. I can protect you if you drink me."*

My hand trembled. "I can't."

"Yes, you can. You need me, Charles. You'll die without me." A transparent hand emerged from the bottle

and touched my arm. *"Think about when you were with Skylar, about that drillmite. Remember how powerless you were. You don't want to go back to that, do you?"*

I shook my head. "I can't. I don't need you anymore."

"Yes, you do," it said more sternly. *"You're a fool if you think you can survive without me. You'll die on your own. You need me. I'm the only one who can protect you, Charles."*

"You're not protecting me; you're infecting me. You're a parasite begging for a host."

"You're making a mistake, Charles. You need me." More transparent hands latched onto me. They grew up my arm.

Instinctively, I threw the bottle to the ground, hands trembling.

The bottle lay there, crumpling, blackening … rotting.

"Charles," said the voice. *"Charles, don't leave me. Don't let me die."*

I shook my head.

"Charles, help me. Please. Don't leave me."

I slowly backed away, each step feeling like I was dragging one-hundred-pound weights.

The water didn't speak anymore. It just rotted like a bad apple. I felt like I was watching my own mother die in front of me; it felt like I was the one who killed her. A piece of myself was gone, rotting. It was dying … But that's just what it wants me to think. It's not dying; it can't die. It's just a bottle of water, and it can't control me any longer; it won't. I won't let it.

I turned and ran into the neighbouring forest, tears filling my eyes.

Chapter 18

I walked through the forest, hands trembling. As usual, I didn't know where I was going. I could hear the wind pushing the leaves out of its way. I could feel its chill, wrapping around me. And I could still hear it—the voice. It was quieter now, but it was still there, calling, wishing, hoping I'd come back.

(*Charles.*)

(*Charles.*)

I don't even know what's real anymore. How long had I been hallucinating? Was it just Liz, or did this start before then? Was Claudette real? Was Stryx real? The time traveller, the young doctor ... the ring? Was the Planet of Shadows even real? It had to be, right? I found the water on this planet, so that much had to be real, right? I don't know if that's comforting or horrifying. I don't know anything anymore.

I guess it's fitting—being in the forest, I mean. There's a reason why literature tends to use the forest as a symbol of loss, or rather, the concept of being lost. Lost in the woods. Alone in the forest. This is where the lost go. This is where we search for purpose, or to embrace the loss.

(*Charles.*)

I let my mind wander, and somehow, it fell to Earth. I miss my home. I miss my sister Ruby, and I miss my parents. I've never thought about this before, life back on Earth, not properly. Why? Is it because it's painful? Is it because the sparkling water didn't want me to? How much of anything that I did or didn't do was truly my decision? All of it? None of it?

From there, my mind drifted to school, of all places. I actually kind of missed it. I miss the teachers, the bullies, and, even though I didn't know her for long, I miss Angela. She was the only person in school who was actually nice to me.

(*Charles.*)

The sparkling water must have really messed me up because I swear I could see Angela in the distance. Her chestnut-brown hair was longer than I remembered, resting on her shoulders in twin braids, although it was a bit messier than before, and she looked a little older. She walked through the forest, and then she stopped and stared at me.

"Charles?" she called. "Oh, my god. Charles, is that you?"

She ran to me, and when she was close enough, she flung her arms around me and hugged me tightly. I clenched up.

"Sorry," she said, releasing her hold on me. "It's just … I haven't seen another human being in such a long time, let alone someone I know."

I didn't say anything. I didn't want to interact with her; she wasn't real. She couldn't be. This was just the sparkling water trying to keep its hold on me.

"Are you okay?" She looked at me. "Say something."

I didn't speak.

(*Charles.*)

"Do you not remember me?" she asked. "I'm Angela. Angela Moon. We met in school. We were going to go see a movie together until … until all this happened."

"You're not real," I breathed, shaking my head.

"Of course I'm real."

"No. You're just a trick to get me to go back, to search the debris, find more of it."

"More of what?" She squinted at me. "Charles, you're shaking. What happened to you?"

(*Charles.*)

She sighed. "Charles, I don't know what happened to you, but I'm really sorry it did. My brother used to deal with hallucinations. Sometimes it's scary. He always felt like he couldn't trust himself. But I said something to him once that he said really helped him. I said to him, 'Just because something's not real, doesn't inherently make it bad. If it's not hurting anyone, does it really matter what's real and what isn't?'" She looked at me calmly. "I'm not going to hurt you, Charles."

Maybe she was right. I may have hallucinated Liz, but it was nice to have a friend, even if he wasn't real. Could Angela be real? She was real to me, maybe that's enough.

"Angela." I smiled, and she smiled back. "How did you get here?"

"Uh, bad popcorn, I think. I was eating it while I was waiting for you at the movie theatre, and then my head started feeling funny. I think I passed out, and then I was here."

"Did you see some strange stuff, like huge, blinking eyes and tons of spiders?"

"Oh, my god, yes, exactly," she gasped.

She paused momentarily, pulling on one of her braids. "Where were you heading?" she asked.

I looked down at my still-trembling hands. "I don't know. Just wandering."

(*Charles.*)

Angela looked at my hands as well. "Are you okay?"

"I hope so. I think it's just withdrawal symptoms. Hopefully, it'll pass."

"Withdrawal from what? Sorry, you don't have to say if you don't want to."

"No, it's fine. I was drinking something I found on this planet. I thought it would help me survive, but it was poisoning me. It was making me see things, hear things. I felt really protective of it, and it made me think things I didn't want to think and do things I didn't want to do. I was dependent on it; I didn't think I could live without it

... and now it's gone, and I don't know if I'm going to be okay."

She was still, watching me shake. "Can I give you a hug?" she asked.

"Sure." I didn't know if that's what I needed; I usually don't like hugs. But she held me tightly, and it grounded me. I wasn't shaking as much, and it was a little easier to focus. It felt nice.

"I'm sorry that happened to you, Charles," she said. "I'm sorry any of this happened. I really wish we had just picked a different day to go see a movie together."

I chuckled. "Then maybe two other people would have been abducted instead of us."

"Could you imagine? What if, right?"

When she let me go, we walked together through the forest, the night cloaking us in darkness. It wasn't completely black, though. The tree leaves glowed in the dark. But soon, we were no longer in a forest; we were in some sort of ruin. There were tall black pillars everywhere, some intact, others cracked and split in two. And now it was only the stars that kept us from complete darkness.

"So, Charles," Angela said. "Can I ask you something?"

"Sure."

She pulled on her braids. "Do you ever think about life back on Earth?"

I looked at her. "Honestly ... no. Today was the first time I've ever really thought about it. You?"

"All the time." She looked down and grinned. "I feel like I can't stop remembering. I dream about how life used to be every night. I miss the times my brother and I would play pool in the basement, and when we'd argue about which one of us was cheating. It was always me; I just liked to push his buttons sometimes. I miss our annual family vacations. This time was my turn to pick the destination." She sighed.

"I guess I miss my sister," I said. "I'm, uh, autistic, and when I was diagnosed, Ruby and I agreed that we would be a team, help each other out. We both kind of get in our own way sometimes. So I would help her to be more autistic, and she would help me to be more allistic. That would kind of split the difference, I guess."

"What's 'allistic'?"

"It just means you're not autistic," I explained.

"Oh, cool. I didn't know there was a word for that."

"Yeah, it's one of those word pairs that most people only know half of. Like cisgender and transgender. It's good, though, because neurodivergence and neurotypicality don't just refer to the presence or absence of autism; they refer to OCD, ADHD, and other things like that. They're not very specific terms. But autism and allism only refer to autism and the lack thereof."

She smiled at me.

"Sorry, I kind of drifted off topic."

"Don't be sorry. I like hearing you explain things. I always thought you were pretty smart." She looked up at the stars. "You know what I miss most, though?"

"What?"

"I miss the culture of Earth. You know, if someone sneezes, you say 'bless you' or 'gesundheit'; when you ask for something, you say 'please', and when you receive something, you say 'thank you'; and you say 'spoiler alert' when you're about to spoil something. I never realized how unique we are as a collective. Planet Earth, the land of humans. There really is nothing like it. You don't really realize that until it's gone. I talked to someone here who didn't even know what *please* meant. Being here is just so difficult, and it's not just because there are dangerous creatures all over the place. Everyone here comes from different backgrounds; it's so hard to just connect with people."

"I don't find it much different actually. Socializing here is just like socializing on Earth. Everyone has all these arbitrary customs and patterns that you have to learn and follow, but once you do that, it gets easier to connect."

"Are you saying I'm being too allistic?" she giggled.

I smiled.

She looked at me and sighed. "I'm really glad I bumped into you, Charles. Just like I did in school, way back when."

"Why did you talk to me back then?" I wondered.

"Because I know what it's like—being bullied. It used to happen to me a lot. In middle school, everyone used to make fun of my hair."

"Why?"

"It used to be really long, down to my hips. Kids would call me Rapunzel, which I took as a compliment at first, but it was the way they said it and how often they said it. They used to say that I used my hair to clean the floor, that it must be dirty and have animals living in it. They made me hate my hair, so much so that I cut it all off. I was bald, and then I got made fun of for that."

I noticed that her braids only reached down to her shoulders.

"The thing is, I love my hair, and I love having long hair. I wish I had never cut it. I wish a hadn't let those kids convince me that the thing I loved about myself was ugly."

"I like your hair," I said.

She smiled. "Thanks. Sometimes that's all it takes. One day, a girl came up to me at school and told me that she liked my hair, and I stopped letting others tell me what I could and couldn't like about myself.

"When it came time for high school, we had to move to a different city for my dad's work. I never saw any of those kids again, but in my new school, I saw you, and you reminded me of myself."

"But why did you want to see a movie with me? Why would you want to see me outside of school? I mean, I always say and do the wrong things, I'm awkward, I'm pasty, I'm—"

"What's wrong with all that?" she chuckled.

"I'm not normal; I'm weird."

"What's so great about being normal? Some of the best inventions and the greatest works of art are made by people who are complete weirdos. It's the perspective those people give to us all, that's what creates normalcy. Everything's weird until it isn't, and then nothing's weird. I mean, look at where we are, Charles. This planet is the furthest you can get from normal. Everyone and everything here is different, but I bet all of us can admit that we've found something beautiful here." She smiled. "The other day, I met a flower who told me a joke and wished me a good day. Do you think *that's* normal?"

I thought about it, disregarding all the negatives and focusing on the good things that have happened here. I've met some nice people: Skylar, Stryx, Claudette; and some strange people, a good strange, like Tom the shape-shifting time traveller, and Sandy, a woman who is psychically linked to another being. Not to mention all the strange places and creatures I've encountered. Angela was right; none of this was normal, and maybe that wasn't necessarily a bad thing.

"Thank you," I told her.

"For what?"

"For showing me a new perspective."

She looked at me and smiled. "Thank you for showing me yours first."

"When did I do that?"

"You always give people a new perspective, Charles."

We both looked up at the night sky. There must have been millions of stars, and I wondered if any of them was Earth.

Angela giggled under her breath.

"What?" I asked.

"I just can't believe you're here, and I'm here. What are the odds that we would be the two people taken from Earth out of everyone else?"

"Incalculable."

"What?"

"The probability of picking two people out of everyone in the world is incalculable, infinite, at least according to an Internet search I did once."

She raised a brow. "Why would you even look that up?"

"You know how the Internet works; you go on it looking for one thing, and you end up finding something completely different."

She smiled. "You see, that's what I mean—weird. That's what makes the world such a beautiful place."

And then there was a sound, like a shifting of rocks.

"What was that?" Angela whispered.

I put my finger to my mouth, telling her to be quiet. I could feel a breeze on the back of my neck ... a warm breeze.

Together, Angela and I slowly turned around. We were met with a monstrous creature nearly twice our combined height. It was coated in a spiky, red shell, like a crab's shell, but that was where the similarities ended. It's a bit difficult to describe, as there's nothing like it on Earth. The creature had six legs, three on either side. They were jagged, each one going straight up into the sky, and then, at a joint, they shot straight down and ended in a single, pointed claw. These claws latched into the ground, keeping the creature balanced. Running my gaze up its body, I noticed how flat it was. The height most definitely came from its legs, as its body was as flat as a disk. And at its second highest point—as its elbows reached higher still—lay its head, with no eyes and no ears, attached to the body by nothing more than a short neck. In place of a mouth was a small hole, no bigger than a coin.

My hands trembled, but they'd never really stopped trembling.

"What is that thing?" Angela whispered.

I shushed her, not wanting to provoke the monster.

"No, it's okay," she said. "I don't think it can hear us. Look, no ears."

She was probably right. The creature was turning its head and eyeing its surroundings, or it would have been if it had eyes.

"Maybe we should just slowly back away," I suggested.

"Good idea." Angela nodded.

As we carefully stepped away, the creature whipped its head in our direction, as if it knew we were there. From the hole in its head, a white tendril emerged, like a really long tongue. It slivered toward Angela and then toward me. It never once touched us, but it slinked around us, in and out, up and down, and then it was sucked back into the hole in the creature's head.

The creature let out a croaking sound, like it was rolling an R and gurgling at the same time. It took a stance and raised its front two legs into the air, making itself look even bigger.

"Run!" I yelled.

Angela and I darted in different directions, but this didn't confuse the creature for a second; it rushed after Angela. I reached for my bottle of sparkling water, but I didn't have it. I got rid of it. How was I going to survive without it?

(*Charles.*)

I picked up a stone from the ground, my hands still trembling. When I let the stone fly, it bounced off the creature's shell, and that got its attention. Now it was coming for me.

I started running, and Angela met back up with me a little farther away. She grabbed my hand and led me through the black pillars of the ruin. Her hands felt clammy, but this was no time to worry about that.

(*Charles.*)

I followed her lead. She looked back at the monster periodically, making sure that we were keeping far enough away from it. But while she was focused on the creature chasing us, I looked ahead and realized we were heading straight for a cliff.

"Angela, stop!" I yelled, but I was too late.

She tripped and fell off the side of the cliff. I held onto her hand, trying to pull her back up. I couldn't even see the bottom of the cliff; it was pitch black. She tried to use her feet to steady herself so she could climb back up, but all she managed to do was kick some small rocks into the blackness below.

As if matters couldn't get any worse, the monstrous creature now loomed over us, breathing out a long croaking sound.

Angela didn't say anything—she couldn't. She was too afraid. The creature croaked and whipped its legs into the air. I yanked Angela's arm as hard as I could, begging for the strength to pull her to safety, but I couldn't do it. I'm not strong enough. I can't do it without the sparkling water.

The creature used its legs to knock me out of the way, and Angela's hand slipped out of mine, and she fell.

(*Charles.*)

Faster than the crack of a whip, the creature sprinted after her. With its pointed claws, it easily scaled down the cliff.

I ran to the edge of the cliff, ignoring any pain I was in.

"Angela!" I yelled.

Nothing.

No scream. No thud. I couldn't even hear the creature climbing down the cliff.

It was silent.

Did that really happen? Did Angela just die because I was too weak to save her?

(*Charles.*)

No. No, I don't believe it. I won't. This is just another trick, a hallucination.

(*Charles.*)

It's like Angela said: What are the odds that the two people from Earth were us? That's impossible. I imagined it, all of it. She's not dead. She's not dead.

(*Charles.*)

But just because I imagined something, doesn't mean it wasn't real.

(*Charles.*)

"Shut up!" I screamed. "Just leave me alone. Please."

I waited, and then ...

(*Charles.*)

The voice, it never goes away. It's a constant reminder that I could have saved her if I still had it.

(*You're nothing without me, Charles.*)

My hands continued to tremble.

***

With my head down and my hands shaking out of my skin, I walked through the glowing trees. Where was I going? I never know.

"*You're pathetic,*" said the voice. It was louder now, stronger. "*You're nothing without me. You deserve to die. You should have stayed with me; you should have used my power. Then she would still be alive. She's dead because you're weak. You need me.*"

"This isn't my fault," I said, trying to make myself believe what I was saying. "You're a parasite. You lured me, addicted me."

"*I did nothing of the sort. You were scared. You drank me because you knew you'd die without me. I did not choose you, Charles, you chose me.*"

"Get out of my head!" I buried my face in my hands.

"*I understand, Charles. I know how you feel. You're scared. You don't trust yourself. Don't you miss how you felt with me? Don't you miss feeling strong, powerful? It's not too late, Charles. You can fix this. Come back to the cabin; I'm still there. Drink me, Charles. You need me. Drink me.*"

"I can't."

"*You can.*"

"No. No, I won't."

"*Why not?*" the voice said sternly.

"I'd rather die than let you control me again."

"*You* will *die!*" the voice screamed. "*You are nothing without me. You don't deserve to have lived this long; I was the one keeping you alive all this time, and you repay me by abandoning me? Just like you abandon everyone else. You deserve to die just like Angela. You deserve to fall off a cliff and have your pieces splattered all over the ground below. You are worthless without me. You deserve to be here, alone. You deserve to die."*

"You don't think I know that?" I yelled. "I didn't ask to be here. I didn't ask to be the most useless creature on this planet. And I *never* asked to be different! You don't think I realize that the only times I've ever been able to protect myself or others have been because of you, that every time someone got hurt or died was because of my shortcomings? You think I don't want to go back and pretend that you haven't been slowly poisoning me this whole time? But it's been you all this time—the voice, the isolation, the anger. You were turning me into someone I'm not. I can't go back. I don't need you … I just want to go home."

The voice didn't respond, and I was alone, tearful in the glowing forest.

None of this was my fault, so why did it feel like it was? Maybe I'm just lying to myself; maybe this was my fault. Stryx warned me, and I didn't listen. That's on me. I chose to drink the sparkling water for as long as I did. Maybe I do deserve everything that's happened to me … No. This isn't my fault; it's whoever's running this planet's fault. That thing has us all trapped here like animals. And it hasn't even bothered to tell us why. It's going to kill us all for its sick experiment, and I have no way of defending myself.

What am I going to do? I'm powerless. I don't have anything that can help me survive on this planet. Everyone I meet seems to have some fantastical ability, and I'm just me. The only thing I'm good at is computers. IT homework was always the thing I was excited to do. It's what I'm good at. But what use is that here? It's not like I have a robot bodyguard or cybernetic enhancements or anything. I wish I were a cyborg, though. Maybe then I could protect myself. And I wouldn't be infected by a parasite I don't understand; it would be a symbiotic relationship with something I've always loved. But that's impossible. I can't turn myself into a cyborg. I'm just me.

I hadn't noticed that I had wandered out of the glowing forest and arrived at a familiar cabin. Multiple lights near the roof illuminated the entrance, and there was a sign next to the door with a red cross on it. This was that young doctor's cabin.

Then I had an idea. I couldn't turn myself into a cyborg, but maybe I knew someone who could.

Chapter 19

"**L**et me get this straight," said Trevor with his snarky English accent. "You want *me* to use my advanced medical science to turn *you* into a cyborg?"

"Yes," I confirmed.

"Are you mad?"

(*Charles.*)

"I don't know, maybe." I scratched my head. "Just ... can you do it or not?"

"Well of course I can do it; look who you're talking to. But the real question is: Are you sure you want me to? You'd be giving up your humanity ... to become a robot. Is that what you want? As smart as I am, I'm not certain I'll be able to reverse that if you go through with it."

"I've always liked computers, and I've lost the thing that protected me before. Why not be protected by something I like—something I understand? Adaptability's the name of the game here, right? This is the only way to keep myself safe."

(*Charles.*)

He made a weird noise. "Matter of opinion, that, one with which I am inclined to disagree. But I won't go so far as to forbid the use of my services." He looked up and shook his head. "Cassie! Bring me a contract, please."

The young girl with neon red-orange hair could be seen through the hoards of sick people in the cabin, peering her little eyes through the half-open backroom door.

"Actually, doctor," she said, "I seem to be having some trouble with one of the patients. I don't suppose you'd lend me a hand?"

Trevor sighed. "Oh, all right." He looked to me. "I implore you to think about this. Once the contract is signed, it is ever-binding. You know that. You should be sure about what you're doing." Then he headed for the backroom to assist Cassie, but not before yelling at a familiar woman who was coughing uncontrollably. "How many times do I have to tell you, cough into the bag? It's no wonder you're still sick. You don't listen, do you? Con-ta-gious, contagious. Not to us, to you. If you don't cough into the bag, you'll just keep reinfecting yourself over and over, then you'll never get well." She coughed again. "Bloody hell! What did I just say? What did I literally just say to you? In the bag! Please. Cor blimey." Then he stormed off into the backroom.

I took some time to think about Trevor's warning, but not too long. My mind was already made up. I had to face facts. I wasn't going to just magically get to go home any time soon. I could be on this planet for years. I'm probably going to die on this planet, and that'll happen sooner rather than later unless I do something about it.

(*Charles.*)

"Hello there," said a man who had just walked in. He was talking to one of the many sick patients here.

The man wore a long brown coat and a rather shiny wristwatch. I knew him. It was Tom the time traveller.

Tom shoved his face right in front of the sick man, fully invading his personal space.

"Can I help you?" the man said, rather weakly.

"Tell me," Tom inquired, "do you have a sore throat, maybe you feel a bit chilly?"

"Yeah, exactly."

He slowly backed away from the sick man. "I should go. I'm so very sorry about your illness."

The man seemed very confused.

I approached Tom. "Hey."

"Hey," he repeated. "Who are you?"

"You don't remember me?"

"Not at all. Why, should I?"

"You told me I would meet someone named Alex soon and about how there was something I had to do here. You said something about a ... a shadow ... shadow-dweller. That's what you called it."

"Whoa, whoa, whoa, spoilers! Don't tell me anything. You're going to ruin the surprise."

"What surprise?"

"Well, you got to experience our meeting for yourself; I'd like for you to extend me the same courtesy."

"What are you talking about? We've already met."

"No, you've already met; I haven't. Your past, my future, that's how time travel works; it's not always in the right order."

I slowly began to wrap my head around this complicated concept.

"So what brings you here?" I asked him.

"Oh, you know." He shrugged. "Stumbled upon something that looked interesting and decided to poke my head in. What about you? This looks like a doctor's office, and you don't seem very sick."

"I came to see if the doctor can turn me into a cyborg," I admitted.

(*Charles.*)

Tom's response surprised me. "Oh, now that is a brilliant idea. I've been meaning to scratch that itch for a while. You know, my best friend is a robot."

"Wait, so you don't think I'm crazy for wanting to be a cyborg?"

"Why would I think that?"

"I don't know, because I'm giving up my humanity or something."

"Well, I could just as easily say you're enhancing your humanity. Human beings walk around with little computers in their pockets all day, but I wouldn't ever call them crazy. The human race possesses one of the most remarkable minds I've ever seen, though it is a tad inclined toward violence against the unknown. But still, it's human to want to integrate. Think of how babies are made—an integration of two innately idiosyncratic individuals. Humans like to mix, mingle, manipulate, multiply, and loads of other things that don't even start with M. I think your wanting to merge with technology is you exercising your natural human inclination.

"Wait, hold on, hang on, shut up, stop," he said abruptly. "You said I said—or I will say—to you about meeting someone named Alex?"

"Yeah," I said slowly. He stared at me intensely. "I still haven't met anyone named Alex, though. The closest I've come is meeting a woman named Sandy whose son's name is Alex."

"Oh, you've met Sandy? How is she?"

"Uh, she seemed okay, I guess. I didn't know you knew her."

He paused for what felt like a long time before saying, "I don't know her."

"Really? It sounds like you do."

"Nope. Never met. Not at all. You'll have to forgive my head; it doesn't work right anymore. Unsafe travel knocked it a bit loose, dangerous but necessary."

"Okay," I said, not fully following.

(*Charles.*)

"You know," he continued, "sometimes there's a reason for meetings like this."

"What do you mean?"

"Maybe the reason you're seeing me again is so you can remember something I'll say ... or something I've already said." He raised his eyebrows.

He may have been right. Now I'm seeing him again, I remember our conversation about the shadow-dweller and Alex far more clearly. Though, none of it made any more sense than it did before.

"Anyway." Tom checked his watch. "I have to be somewhere in about twenty seconds, so I'll see you later ... or I guess, for you, I won't." He then shrank into the form of a small toad and hopped away.

(*Charles.*)

Trevor returned briskly from the backroom, holding a large contract.

"Okay," he said. "Are you absolutely sure you want to go through with this?"

"I am."

"All right, then you'll need to sign this. It states that, in exchange for my services, any property you currently possess and/or will come to possess in the future now belong to me, and I may use said property as I see fit." He handed me a pen.

I signed almost immediately. This signature would change my life; I knew that. But I wasn't afraid. My life changed ever since I got to this planet, and I had to protect myself, whatever it takes, no matter the cost.

"All right," Trevor continued, smiling. "Now, just follow me into the backroom, and we'll crack on."

I did as he said, and we both walked into one of the backrooms. The room had a little bed in the centre and tons of medical equipment that I couldn't name for the life of me. Cassie stood next to the bed, pulling her neon red-orange hair into an updo and tapping the bed with her hand to get me to sit. I obliged.

Trevor looked at me. "Right, I'm just going to give you a quick once over before we start." He pulled out a card-shaped object from his pocket, climbed up onto the bed, and ran it over my arms and around my face. Then he scrunched his brow. "No, that can't be right. Cassie, come have a look at this."

"Certainly, doctor." She climbed up onto the bed and took the card from Trevor, running it over my body as well. "Oh, feck."

"So I've not gone mad, then?" the doctor confirmed.

"Certainly not, doctor. This is one of the worst cases I've seen."

"What is it? What's wrong?" I asked.

"You have cintin poisoning," Doctor Trevor explained.

"What's that?"

Cassie elaborated. "It means your blood has high levels of toxicity due to cintin water ingestion—it's a sparkly, twinkly water."

(*Charles.*)

"Not just high levels of toxicity," Trevor added, "extremely high levels. How much of it did you drink?"

"I don't know, probably a lot," I admitted.

"Bloody hell, I am honestly surprised you are still sane."

"That's debatable," I muttered.

Trevor smiled. "Yeah, I suppose it is."

"Doctor," Cassie started. "You do realize that his signature on the contract is now null and void until we get his condition under control?"

He sighed and shook his head. "Yeah, I knew it was too good to be true. Right, get me a detox and a bucket, Cassie."

"Of course, doctor." She jumped off the bed and fished around the room for a bucket and a bottle of orange liquid.

She handed them up to me. "Here you are."

When I took them, Doctor Trevor said, "Drink that, and it should clear your blood of any toxins."

"What's the bucket for?" I wondered.

"The toxins need to go somewhere, now, don't they?" Cassie answered.

(*Charles.*)

I cautiously drank the liquid. It was lumpy, and it had a faint, sweet taste that failed to mask how disgusting it was. When I finished, Cassie took the bottle back, and she and the doctor stared at me.

"Now what?" I asked, and immediately afterward, I violently vomited into the bucket for the next five minutes. It felt horrible, and the vomit smelled even worse than it felt, but after that, I never heard the voice again.

"I'll have that," said Cassie, taking the bucket away.

Doctor Trevor ran his card-shaped device up and down my body again. "Looks good. How are you feeling?"

I looked at my hands. They weren't trembling anymore. "I feel good," I said.

"Good. And do you still stand by your signature on my contract?"

"I do."

He grinned. "Brilliant! Oh, just smashing!"

"Calm down, doctor," said Cassie.

"Yes, of course." He cleared his throat and looked at me. "Have you given much thought to what type of cybernetic enhancements you want exactly?"

"Not really," I said. "What would you recommend?"

He grinned again. "Well, I was thinking detachable arms that can be remotely controlled with a thought; laser beam implants in your retinas; two small thrusters in your back enabling flight, as well as a flight stabilizer; and of course, the standard enhanced strength and durability."

"Doctor Trevor's always wanted to do this sort of thing," Cassie explained as she put a lid over my bucket of vomit.

"Okay, well, that all sounds great," I said. "As long as it will help me defend myself."

"Oh, yes, of course." Trevor nodded. "Also, if I may, I'd like to implant a computer chip in your brain that will enable you to convert, translate, upload, and download digital and biological data."

"Sure, sounds good."

"Fantastic. Let's get started, then. Cassie! Anesthetic please!"

"Feck! You don't have to yell, doctor, I'm right here," said Cassie, readying a syringe.

"Sorry, Cassie. Force of habit."

Cassie pulled up a stool to stand on, so she could be tall enough to reach my arm. I supposed that was a steadier platform than the surface of the bed.

"Are you ready?" she asked me.

"Yes." I nodded.

"All right, then, lie down for me."

I did so, and she injected me with the drug.

"Now, if you could count backward from one hundred for me," she said.

"Why?"

"It lets us know ..."

I was out before Cassie even finished her sentence.

***

My eyelids split open, and I slowly regained consciousness. The first thing I saw was Cassie, standing on a stool and staring at me. "He's awake, doctor," she said.

"Oh, good," he sighed. "That was a tough one, weren't it? Hop off the stool, Cassie. Let me have a look at him."

"Yes, doctor." Cassie got down from the stool, and Trevor climbed up. During the switchover, I sat up.

"Easy," said the doctor. "You might be a bit dizzy."

"No, I feel fine," I said.

"Good, good." Trevor nodded, looking at Cassie. Then he retrieved something from his pocket and looked back at me. "This is a pen."

"I can see that."

"Good. How about now?" He threw the pen at my face, but I caught it before it could hit me. There was a red circle around the pen, which appeared immediately when it was thrown. The circle was accompanied by some text that read: "Threat Neutralized". Then the circle turned green and disappeared along with the text.

Trevor continued. "All right, reflexes and targeting systems are operational." He pulled a metal briefcase out from under the bed and walked over to the back of the room, facing the wall.

"Cassie," he said. "I need a boost, please."

"Of course, doctor."

Cassie walked over to him and crouched down, and when Trevor climbed on top of her, she lifted him into the air. At his new height, Trevor touched his hand to the wall and a door materialized there in response.

"You have an invisible door?" I asked.

"It was here when we moved into the cabin," Cassie explained.

"Rather convenient actually," Trevor added. "It's a staff-use-only situation. I'm sure you can understand why we keep it invisible."

"Some of our patients can be a little rash and tend to be very bold in the throws of illness," said Cassie. "We wouldn't want them to know how easy it is to escape, especially given how young the doctor and I are. We're not as old as we used to be; we wouldn't be able to stop someone from running off in a fit of delirium, for instance."

I nodded.

"Right," Trevor said, climbing down from Cassie's shoulders and opening the invisible door. "Off we pop. Let's go test out the rest of your abilities."

I got out of bed and immediately fell on the floor.

"Oh, sorry," Trevor said. "I must not have calibrated the gyro sensors properly. Cassie, would you fix that for me?"

"Of course, doctor." Cassie walked over to me and took my hand. She pulled back my skin like a sliding door, revealing a labyrinth of circuitry. She tampered with it for a few seconds and then pulled my skin back over my hand.

"Okay, all set," she said. "Try standing now."

I stood, and sure enough, I could balance again.

"There we are," said Trevor. "Now, come with me."

I walked over to him, but before we went outside, Cassie asked, "Will you be needing me for anything else, doctor?"

"Uh, no, I should be fine with him. You just tend to our other patients, yeah?"

"Certainly, doctor."

"Oh, and if you see that eejit of a woman who chooses not to cough in the bag we gave her, give her a good bash on the head for me, will you?"

Cassie grinned. "My pleasure, doctor."

And with that, Trevor and I went outside. He closed the door behind us, and it remained fully invisible from this side despite now being visible from the inside.

We stood in an open field full of greenery. The wind brushed across the blades of grass, and the tall trees of the forest surrounded the area.

"All right," Trevor started, laying his briefcase down on the ground and opening it. "Let's start with some target practice. I'm going to throw a plastic disk, and you are going to destroy it with a laser beam from your eyes."

"Okay. How do I do that?" I asked.

"It's rather simple, really. All your functions are neurologically mapped to your brain, so using them is as simple as moving your arm; you don't necessarily have to think about it, you just do it."

I nodded.

He took a disk from his briefcase and threw it. As it soared through the air, a green circle appeared around it, probably some sort of targeting system. I squinted my eyes and a green laser beam shot from them, destroying the disk.

"Fantastic," Trevor exclaimed. "I've designed you quite well, haven't I?"

"Yeah, that was pretty cool." I couldn't help but agree.

"Let's kick it up a notch, shall we?"

He threw two disks this time, and I shot them easily with a green laser.

He grinned. "I'd say that works quite well. Right, let's move on to your next function." He took a small, brown ball from the briefcase and threw it into the distance. "I want you to fetch me that ball without moving from that spot."

I was confused but excited to see what would happen, so I gave it a try. I reached out, reaching for the ball, and then my arm detached at the elbow. It soared silently through the air, retrieved the ball, and then reattached itself to the rest of my arm.

"Wow, that's amazing," I said.

"Innit, though?" Trevor looked like he could hardly contain himself. "Anyway, um, if you could just detach your other arm as well, just to make sure that one works, too."

I detached the other arm and flew it around in circles for a bit. I couldn't believe how easy it was to control, just as easy as it would be were it still attached to me.

"Okay, fully functional," said Trevor. "Moving on."

I reattached my arm and nodded.

"There are thrusters in your back. If you activate them, you should be able to fly around as freely as a bird."

I immediately gave this a try. I could feel the thrusters emerging from my back. I slowly rose into the air and floated just above the ground. The thrusters were quiet; I could barely hear their hum. I flew around so naturally; it was almost easier than walking.

"How come the thrusters don't burn my shirt off?" I asked.

"Why would they?" Trevor wondered. "Don't tell me the thrusters on your world are still combustible."

"Are they not meant to be?"

"Oh, bloody hell. What sort of backward planet do you come from? Do you know how dangerous combustible thrusters are? Next, you're going to tell me that you still perform chest compressions to restart someone's heart." I was silent, but he must have read something on my face. "Oh, come on, you don't, do you? Chest compressions? Really? You risk breaking bones just to restart someone's heart?" He looked away. "I can't."

I rolled my eyes and smiled. "If it's not combustible, then what fuel do the thrusters run on?"

"Fuel? What are you on about? They're self-sustaining. You don't have that either?"

I shook my head. "Not for things like thrusters."

"Blimey, how do you even survive? Remind me never to visit your planet. It'd be like living in the bleeding Dark Ages. Where were you from again?"

"Earth."

"No, the intergalactic name, obviously."

"I don't know ..."

"Oh, right, I forgot. You're from one of *those* planets." He shook his head. "You're not even a member of the Intergalactic Union yet."

I chuckled and returned to the ground.

"All right, let's just move on," he continued. "I've implanted a chip in your brain that will allow you to convert, translate, upload, and download any digital or biological data from a server or hard drive. Basically, you can convert your thoughts into digital files and store them on a computer and vice versa. You can also use it to tune in to different radio waves, although you probably won't hear anything too interesting here. But try it out anyway, just to make sure it works."

As soon as I tried it, I heard crackling at different frequencies, but then I heard something I wasn't expecting. It was a voice, a very deep and demonic voice.

"I apologize for how long this is taking," it said. "I didn't expect these creatures to survive for as long as they have. Not to mention The Third Event has hit a small delay."

"I hear something," I said to Trevor.

"You do?" He sounded kind of shocked. "What is it? What do you hear?"

I shushed him, as I could hear another voice answering. It sounded very similar to the first voice. "Perhaps you should stop underestimating these creatures and start overestimating them. Need I remind you of our various defeats in the other dimensions?"

"No, I remember quite clearly," the first voice said. "Though, I'd hardly consider Dimension-003 a failure. We may have lost the Faction Leader there, but they did accomplish the task."

"And they did so by appropriately estimating the threat. Our species grows smaller by the day. The abeedoids are hunting us at every corner of the multiverse, and the interdimensional traveller keeps gathering more people. I fear he's planning something disastrous. We need you to regroup with us in Dimension-005, but not without the data. Your work is vital; we cannot afford for you to fail."

"I won't. I just need a bit more time."

"We don't have time. Creating this planet was an ambitious endeavour from the start. It would have been easier to experiment on the creatures the way we did in Dimension-003."

"The Planet of Shadows provides a more natural environment, ergo it produces more accurate results. The hybrids your faction created in Dimention-003 were barely functional. I mean to produce infallible data when this is done."

"Regardless, we need that data soon. Our enemies will not wait for us to be prepared."

"I understand."

There was a pause, and then, the first voice spoke again. "If I could be allowed the privilege to confide in you?"

"You may."

"Thank you ... I find myself feeling an emotion that I have not felt in quite some time."

"We all feel it, comrade: fear. Our enemies are far more formidable than we once believed, and our chances of victory shrink with every passing day, which is why it is imperative that you finish your work and regroup with us, before it's too late."

"I shall do my best."

"For all our sakes, I hope your best is enough. Now, on to other matters. Once you regroup with us in Dimension-005—"

"Hold on. I apologize, but it appears someone is listening in on our conversation. Some of the creatures on this planet are so advanced; it's difficult to keep a secure channel without one of them figuring out how to tap into it. Allow me just a moment."

With that, a crackling noise blocked out the rest of the conversation.

"Well," said Trevor. "What did you hear?"

I hesitated. "It ... sounded like the voice we all heard when we arrived on this planet, but there were two of them."

"Two? Interesting." He smiled to himself. "I can't wait for the opportunity to make them sign my contract. If they are the beings that brought us here, and if they sign my contract, I could take possession of this whole bloody planet. I think I'd get them sick myself for that."

I wasn't really listening to him. What I'd heard worried me. The voices spoke of The Third Event, and if I remembered what Tom said correctly, I needed to stop this shadow-dweller thing before it activated The Third Event.

I took a breath and elected to mask my anxieties in favour of completing the explanation of my new, cybernetically enhanced body.

"What's next?" I asked.

Trevor pulled out a small USB-like device from his briefcase. "I need you to download what's on here."

I thought about downloading it and watched a floating green progress bar fill to one hundred percent. I then thought about what I'd downloaded and realized it was a rather irritating song played on what sounded like a piano.

"What is this?" I asked.

"My favourite song. It's beautiful. I listen to it every day."

He and I obviously had very different tastes in music.

"Now," he said. "Upload the song back into the device."

I uploaded it and watched the floating progress bar count to one hundred again.

"All right, looking good." He reached into his briefcase for another USB-like device. "On this is everything you need to know about your new body. Just download it and always keep it in your memory. If you ever break down, with this, you'll know how to fix yourself."

I downloaded it, and with that, Trevor put everything back into the briefcase and closed it shut.

"And we're done," he said. "Pleasure doing business with you, my good sir."

"Likewise," I said.

Then the invisible door opened again, and Cassie poked her head out. "Doctor," she said, "there's a situation in here I need your help with."

"Be right there, Cassie." Trevor picked up his briefcase and looked at me. "I have to go, but before I do, remember that you are still about sixty percent human. That means your memory won't be quite as efficient as a computer's; it can be corrupted far more easily. I suggest finding an external hard drive to store some of your more important thoughts on. I wouldn't worry about it too much now, but in future, you won't be able to store everything in that head of yours."

"Um, doctor, please hurry," said Cassie.

"Coming." He ran over to her with the briefcase in hand.

"Thanks, Trevor," I said.

"What did you call me?" he asked.

"Trevor. Isn't that your name?"

"It's *Doctor* Trevor."

"Oh, sorry. Doctor Trevor."

He smiled. "I'm just funning you."

"Your what?"

"I'm joking."

"Doctor, please," Cassie urged.

"Right," he said. "I'll see you when I see you, Charles."

They both ran into the cabin before anything else could be said, and I went on my way.

Chapter 20

The wind brushed against my face as I silently soared through the air with my new flight capabilities. It was a bit more difficult than I'd imagined. Even though flying felt like second nature to me, it was still hard to avoid all the tree branches around. It's kind of like the difference between running and cross-country running—running is something any novice can do, but cross-country running takes practice. As for why I was flying at tree level and not soaring high above them, well, that would defeat the purpose of practice, wouldn't it? I had to get good at manoeuvring in the air. The whole point of getting these cybernetic enhancements was to be able to protect myself, so this all needs to become intuitive to me.

Things weren't going too well, though, as I was soon smacked in the face by an unnoticed tree branch, and I fell into the tree's embrace. Clutching one of the branches, I pulled myself up and sat atop it.

"Ow," I muttered.

I opened and closed my hands repeatedly. I could hear the hum of the electronics coursing through them, but maybe that was just in my head. I wonder what my family will think when I get back home ... if I get back home. It's been so long, they probably think I'm dead. I've probably become a cold case. What would they think if I showed up ten years older and with cybernetic enhancements, talking about some place called the Planet of Shadows? Would they even believe me?

My stomach growled loudly. I guess even though I'm part robot, I still have to eat. The tree I was in bared no fruit, but a neighbouring tree bared a plump, yellow berry. I detached my arm and had it fly over to pick the berry and bring it back to me. My arm reattached itself, and I bit into the juicy fruit.

Chewing slowly, I wondered what the plan was now. It's not like I'm getting off this planet any time soon. Do I just continue to wander like before?

Then, a dark, floating, ghost-like creature emerged from the trees. My robot brain placed a red circle around it with the word "hostile" above. I know everything there is to know about my new body, thanks to the files that Trevor had me download. The chip in my brain scans my memories and experiences in order to predict with ninety-percent accuracy whether the thing I'm facing is a friend or a foe. In other words, if my brain tells me this thing is hostile, it's probably right.

I silently flew to the ground and walked away, hoping it wouldn't notice me and that I wouldn't have to get into a fight. I didn't take my eyes off it—its small, hunched body; its unmoving eyes, always looking straight ahead.

With my eyes locked on the creature and my feet taking me in the opposite direction, I inevitably bumped into something and fell to the ground. When I looked to see what I'd bumped into, I realized it was a man with whom I was very familiar, a man with droopy rectangular ears and a glistening cerulean complexion. He carried a basket filled with berries.

"Skylar?" I said, shocked.

"Charles. Long time no see." He held out his hand to help me up. "I know you don't like handshakes, but I hope you'll make an exception this time."

I smiled. "That's okay. I can get up on my own," and I did so. "Thanks, though."

He smiled back. "I'd love to catch up, Charles, but we shouldn't be here. That thing up there is pretty dangerous." He pointed to the creature I was originally moving away from. "We should find a safer place to chat."

"What is that thing?"

"A krogramoq. They're soul collectors."

"Like, they eat souls?"

"No, just collect. It won't bother us if we don't bother it, so let's go."

I nodded, and we slowly walked away, unbeknownst to the creature.

"So, what have you been up to?" Skylar asked while we walked through the thick forest.

"A lot," I sighed. "I'm still alive, though. That's the main thing."

"So I see. I'm glad. I've always hoped the best for you."

I smiled. "Where's the rest of the group?"

"Well, Trish ended up leaving shortly after you did."

"Yeah, I ran into her."

"You did? How is she?"

I told him about what she did to Claudette's husband and how she hit her head and lost her memory.

"Wow," said Skylar. "I suppose, in a way, that's for the best. Trish seemed very confused and distracted when she left. Maybe now that she can't remember, she'll be more at peace."

"What about Waxton?" I asked. "Is he still around?"

"Yeah, he's with our new recruit. I'm actually on my way to meet up with them." Skylar smiled. "And speak of the devil."

A man approached us—a rather cartoonish-looking man with a long black coat and two katanas sheathed and mounted on his back.

"Charles," said Skylar, "this is—"

"Stryx!" I finished.

"Yo, dude. Whaddup?" He greeted.

"I take it you two have already met, then," Skylar chuckled.

"Yeah, man, I helped this lil' dude out a little while ago," Stryx explained.

"How are Tri and Nine?" I asked him.

"They're good. I see you're finally acknowledging them."

I smiled. "You know I still can't see them."

"Nah, you just think ya can't. Tri, don't start. It ain't their fault; they're being influenced."

I looked to Skylar. He seemed just as confused by Stryx's friends as I first was.

"Charles," said a small man with a single eye and antenna, poking his head out from behind Stryx. "Thought I never see thou again."

"Hey, Waxton," I greeted.

"Stryx," said Skylar, "did you manage to get rid of the cintin water we found?"

"Sure did. Good thing, too, stuff's dangerous." Stryx looked to me. "Speaking of ..." Then he stopped, his eyes following something in the air, like he were looking at a buzzing fly, but there was nothing there. "Sorry, what was I saying? Right, uh, how did things go with your supply of cintin water? Hope you went off the stuff after finishing it."

"Wait, Charles, you were drinking cintin water?" Skylar butt in. "Since when?"

"Shortly after I left you guys," I said. "And, uh, you were right, Stryx. My bracelet did nothing, and it got really bad. But I'm off it now, for good."

"I'm sorry, man," said Stryx. "That must have been rough. That crap can really sneak up on you." He looked to his left. "Told you. No, no buts. He said it himself; I was right." He looked back at me. "So what are all these electronics in ya?"

I scrunched my brow. "How do you know about that?"

"I can—will you shut up? I know it's Charles; I can see him. You don't have to say it every five seconds. Sorry, where was I? Right, I can see 'em, your robot parts."

"What, like X-ray vision?"

"Sure, yeah. You didn't know I could do that?"

"No."

"Oh ... well, I can." He looked me up and down. "That's some pretty advanced tech inside ya."

"How advanced?" Skylar wondered. "Describe it."

"Do ya one better." Stryx unsheathed one of his swords. It glowed pink. He waved it in front of me from top to bottom. After this, my skin became translucent. All the technology, all the beeping lights and metal joints, became visible.

"Wow," said Waxton, "very advanced."

"How did this happen?" said Skylar. "Or were you always like this?"

"A doctor—Trevor—he helped me do it," I explained.

"Good question," said Stryx. "Why would ya want all them electronics in ya?"

"Without the sparkling water," I said, "I had to find some way of protecting myself. I don't know. This just seemed like the best way, I guess."

Stryx sheathed his sword and my skin returned to normal.

"Well, as you said," Skylar weighed in, "your still alive. I suppose that's all that matters."

I nodded.

"I see ya got the berries." Stryx pointed to Skylar's basket.

"Yes, I did. We're all set."

"Set for what?" I asked.

"We're heading out to confront the person running this planet," Skylar said. "Hopefully we'll be able to stop them and get everyone back home."

"Wait, you ... you found who brought us here?"

"Yes and no. Do you remember those ruins we went to way back when, to help feed the elderly?"

"Yeah."

"Well, Waxton here was walking around there some time ago, and he noticed a dark, shadowy creature with some sort of strange device. He grew sleepy, and by the time he awoke, the creature and its device were gone. That was when that big storm hit."

"Same thing happen at quake," Waxton added. "Same creature, same device. It make me sleep."

Stryx added his thoughts. "We think this creature's the one that brought about the storm and the quake, and if it can do that, there's a good chance it's running the planet as well. Problem is, we don't know where it comes from or where it goes."

"That's why we're going to stay camped in those ruins until it shows up again," said Skylar.

I considered what they were saying. The creature sounded familiar. "It's a shadow-dweller."

"What's that?" said Stryx. "I'm not familiar."

"I don't know. A time traveller told me about it. He said that the shadow-dweller runs the planet and causes The Events, but in order to do so, it has to come to the planet's surface. He said I'm supposed to do something about it before it unleashes The Third Event."

"Well, I don't know about any of that," said Skylar, "but we'll gladly accept your help, if you're offering."

"Yeah. I'll help." I didn't hesitate. This was the last thing I should have been doing if my goal was to stay alive, but when a time traveller tells you to do something, it sort of becomes fate, doesn't it? And if I can stop this, if I can end all of this and go home, I have to try.

"Good. Then we go," said Waxton.

"One question, though," I said. "If the device makes you sleep like Waxton says, what's to stop us from sleeping through the whole thing and missing this creature's arrival?"

"That's where I come in, lil' dude," Stryx answered, tapping his katanas. "All it'll take is an insomnia charm from my blades, and we'll be fine." He looked to his right.

"You were on vacation when I learned it, 'member? ... I forgot. Do I really have to tell you everything, Nine? I do live a life when you're not around."

"All right, then," said Skylar. "Let's get going."

We all travelled together through the forest. If our suspicions were correct and our plan was sound, then this will be my final adventure on the Planet of Shadows.

Chapter 21

We had arrived at the sandy, derelict ruins some time ago. Together, Skylar, Waxton, Stryx, and I had spent many days and many nights in this barren place. We were all drained of energy and drained of hope. We already had to fight off a drillmite attack, and now, we were running out of food. All we had left was a small amount of water—left over from a few nights ago when we happened to find some—and a raging campfire, around which we were all seated. Stryx's katanas were wedged into the ground, projecting a pink circle around us which cast the insomnia charm. So even though we were tired, we weren't sleepy.

"Skylar," I said, "maybe we should call this off. I mean, we've been here for days. We don't even know if this shadow-dweller creature will come."

"Waxton said it would," he said quickly.

"Waxton only knows what he saw. That doesn't mean the creature will come back. We don't know that."

"Charles, you said it yourself, about the time traveller; he said the same thing as Waxton."

"He also had to look in a book to remember my name and what timeline he was in. He was scatterbrained. He actually said his head wasn't working right because he time travelled unsafely or something. Maybe he didn't remember the events properly."

"Agreement," Waxton weighed in. "We find another way. This madness."

Skylar sighed. "Stryx? What do you think?"

Stryx shrugged. "Sorry, man. I'm with mono-eye and robot-man."

Skylar looked at all of us, studying all our faces. "So that's it, then? A few rough days, and you all want to give up?"

"It ain't giving up, man," said Stryx. "This just ain't the best use of our time. How long do you expect us to wait?"

"As long as it takes."

"And what if it takes another week?" I said. "Another month? A year? Skylar, we can't do this forever."

He paused. "On my planet, there is a man, the most beautiful man I've ever met, and he is pregnant with our child ... or he was. That kid's ten years old now. I've already missed so much of their life. Look, you all know me; I'm very level-headed. But I think about that all the time. I think about how much I love my family. I think about it so much that it burns, and sometimes, all I want to do is scream, get angry. There is someone to blame for all of this. This was no accident; someone took me away from my family. And I want to be angry; I should be angry

... But that won't get me back to them. So I channel my pain, that burn I feel for loving them so much, and I put it toward getting back to them.

"We know that creature will eventually show up here. Charles heard someone say so, and Waxton saw it with his own eye. That's good enough for me. So I will wait for as long as I must, and if I'm the only one who'll wait, so be it. But I'd like to believe that you all have reason to go back to your homes as well. I'd like to believe you won't give up on that because it's difficult or hopeless. Hope's not something that's supposed to be easy to see. If it were, you wouldn't have to believe in it; you'd just know it's there. I'm going to wait, and I'm going to hope, for my family."

There was silence.

"Brother and I," Waxton started. "We fight, in last moments. Big fight ... I sorry. Want forgiveness, but not if here. I stay with thou, Skylar. I hope."

"Thank you," said Skylar. "What about the rest of you? Do you still want to call it?"

I pondered, maybe for longer than I should have. "I just want all this to be over. I want to be okay. So much has happened to me on this planet, and I don't know if I'll ever be able to just move past it and go back to my regular life ... It won't even be my regular life; it'll be a decade later. Everyone I know will be older. Ruby will be older, maybe she married Maxine, maybe they started a family together. And Angela ... I don't even know if ... I don't know if she was ever really here, if she really did die. Maybe she wasn't here. I hope she wasn't. Maybe I could see her again. I won't be able to move past any of this until it's over. So I think I'll stay, too. I'm with you, Skylar."

We all looked to Stryx.

"Well, the popular vote flipped real quick, didn't it?" he said. "Life ain't changing for me once I'm off this rock. I'll still be a member of the Tristan Corps—same job, different world. But I'll stick with the majority on this one ... Do you want a vote, Tri? All right, vote, then. Waste of time; you're outnumbered anyway. And where'd Nine go?" Stryx looked to us. "Did any of you see where ... of course you didn't; you never do. Guess that's reason enough to stay as well. Once we find who's running this planet, I can make them get these chips out of everyone's brains."

"Stryx, I don't know what you're talking about," said Skylar. "No one's chipped."

"Yes, you are. That's how you can read my mind and why none of you can see Tri and Nine. Whoever's running this place, they've got you round their finger, man. But we're going to stop 'em, all of us."

Skylar sighed and decided to just drop it.

"So, if we're staying here," I started, "we're going to need to find more food. What we have will barely last another meal."

Stryx came to his feet. "Sounds fun. I'll go into the forest and look for berries."

"Wait," I said. "Your swords are projecting the insomnia charm. They need to stay here; you can't take them with you. If anything attacks you in the forest, you'll be defenceless."

"Well, looks like I'll need a bodyguard, then. You offering?"

I agreed, and together, we walked into the forest with a basket, in search of food. We couldn't stay away too long. Without Stryx's swords, all our lost sleep would eventually catch up with us, and we would collapse from exhaustion. Luckily, the charm's effects linger for a little while.

Stryx pointed out ripe berries and I retrieved them with my detachable arms, and we continued this method of berry picking throughout our walk.

"Stryx," I said, "can I ask you something?"

"Just did, lil' man, but you can ask somthin' else."

I smiled. "Before we left the campfire, you said that your life would be no different if you weren't on this planet."

"Yep. What of it?"

"Don't you have any family back home?"

"Nah, my family's all gone." He grinned, not the reaction I was expecting.

"What happened to them?"

"Uh … when I was little, I wanted to be an artist, but my folks didn't approve. They thought it was a waste of time, you know, that I was better off applying my talents elsewhere. They wanted me to fight, so I could protect my tiny village. You see, there were other Tristan Corps members but none in my village. So if there's trouble, it takes a while for help to come. But I was no fighter; I wanted to make art. Someone else could do the fighting." He looked up. "And then a hurricane broke through, first one in decades. It tore through the village, and the Tristan Corps didn't make it in time. Lotta people died in that storm, including my folks. Then I was alone. That's when I met Tri and Nine. We kept meeting each other on the road, a few times, chatting and whatnot. They convinced me to join the Tristan Corps and learn to fight, for my folks. They convinced me to be there to protect the little guy, to be what my tiny village needed when the storm hit. That's my life now. Same life no matter where I am."

"But what about being an artist?" I asked. "Don't you still want to do that?"

"Yeah, but ... meh, I ain't no good at it anyway."

"Then that's your reason to go back."

"Huh?"

"Your reason to return home, so you can get good at it, so you can have the chance to be who you want to be and merge that with who you already are."

He shook his head. "I dunno, man."

"It sounds to me like you've spent your whole life assuaging your parents' wishes. And you've done it well; you've saved my life, multiple times. When this is all over,

I think you should try doing something for yourself. Be the artist you always wanted to be."

He smiled and looked up into the purple night sky. "Y'know, that idea ain't half bad."

***

Stryx and I returned to the others with a bag full of berries, and on the next day, Skylar and Waxton found some more water. Many days and nights passed, and we all tried our hardest to keep our spirits up.

And then it happened.

There were flashing lights in the distance, and then a crack in reality appeared—a swirling, purple portal. From it emerged a six-foot-tall, pitch-black creature with sharp teeth and red squinted eyes. Its heart was blacker than the night, and it was half submerged in its chest. Black blood flowed throughout its veins, and those veins lay atop its skin. My robotic brain revealed a red circle around the creature, captioned: "Dangerous".

The creature carried a metal briefcase. It placed it on the ground, and from it emerged a monitor with a holographic keyboard. The creature placed its hands on the keyboard and got to work.

"Hey!" said Skylar, getting the creature's attention. "Are you the one who's trapped us all on this planet?"

The creature glanced at us quickly and then raised its hand, turning a shadow cast by a nearby tree into a solid, shadowy wall. The wall was launched at Skylar, and it knocked him over.

The rest of our little team all knew what to do now.

I took to the air and shot a laser beam from my eyes at the creature. Its response was another shadow creation, this time more liquid than solid. The creation resembled octopus tentacles. They surrounded the creature, blocking my laser beams from making contact.

Stryx drew one of his swords from the ground. This made the charm slightly weaker, and as a result, I felt a bit groggy, but I could still fight. He swung his sword and cut one of the shadowy tentacles in two, but it simply grew back after absorbing more shadows. He chopped some more tentacles in two, but the same thing happened. Stryx couldn't fight a living shadow.

As for Waxton, the tentacles stretched after him, and he avoided them mostly, but there wasn't much else he could do.

Throughout all this, the creature continued to type on its keyboard while glancing at our struggle with its tentacle defence every now and then. But now it had finished, and with a smile on its face, it returned the monitor to the briefcase, picked it up, and started walking back to the portal, all while keeping its shadowy tentacles on the defensive.

"Charles!" Stryx yelled. "Cover me; use your lasers."

I obeyed his command. Though this didn't stop the creature from leaving, it did occupy the tentacles enough for Stryx to ready a spell of some sort. A pink aura shone around his sword.

Then Skylar rejoined the fray, throwing rocks that were too small for the tentacles to block. These rocks did nothing but slow the creature down a bit, though that was better than nothing.

Stryx lunged his sword skyward and then slashed it forward, propelling a half-moon-shaped beam of pink light at the creature. This tore its tentacle defence to shreds, leaving the shadowy creature defenceless.

Stryx moved in for an attack, but the creature faced him and caught him by the neck. It plunged a fist into his gut and threw him aside.

Skylar and Waxton moved in as well, but they didn't get very close. They were thwarted by large shadow balls, conjured up by the creature and launched in their direction.

The creature was escaping into its portal. I couldn't allow that, especially if what Tom had told me was true. This was my last chance to stop this, to go home, my last chance to see my planet, my species, my family. This creature had easily defeated our entire group. It was up to me now; I had to stop it.

I flew as fast as I could, trying to catch the creature before it could escape. It was already halfway through the portal. I had to make it; I had to. This won't turn out the way it did with Angela. I'm not powerless anymore. I have to make it. I reached out my hand, and by the tip of my longest finger, I touched the portal. Then the portal closed shut, and everything went dark.

THIRD EVENT
PLAGUE

Chapter 22

There was a humming sound. It surrounded me. I opened my eyes and found that I was surrounded by machines. They were nothing like any machines I'd seen before. Some looked like long, metal poles with flashing lights, and others were floating spheres with narrow screens on them.

I lay on the ground, a very strange ground. It looked like a fluffy, white cloud, but it didn't feel fluffy, or wet, or however one would expect a cloud to feel. It felt like a flat plane of concrete.

I pushed myself off the ground and into a kneeling position. My gaze twitched around, noticing the black, starry sky and the fact that this cloud I was on seemed to float in an endless, starry space.

Then there was a sudden sound, like someone had dropped a heavy box. My gaze whipped toward it, and I saw the creature, the one that escaped through the portal. It didn't look as menacing as before; it almost seemed … afraid? I couldn't read its face. It breathed heavily.

"How did you get here?" it said in a deep, demonic voice.

I slowly came to my feet, feeling a little disoriented. Stryx's insomnia charm must have been starting to wear off. "I don't know," I said. "Same way you did, I guess. Where are we?"

"That is none of your concern." The creature moved toward one of the machines. A holographic keyboard appeared next to it, and the creature began to type. "I am a creature of my word. In the beginning, I said that the last survivor would be granted passage back to their home world." The creature pressed a key, and a light shot out of the machine, projecting a purple portal behind me. "Congratulations. You are the last survivor."

I looked back at the swirling, purple portal, and then back at the creature. "What do you mean 'last survivor'? I'm not the last survivor. Skylar, Stryx, Waxton, they're all still alive; I just saw them."

"They're not alive anymore, surely. According to my data, they, along with every other living creature on the Planet of Shadows, have succumbed to The Third Event."

I had to really dig for it, but I vaguely remembered seeing something ... words ... "Plague. What plague? What happened to them?"

"The only thing you need concern yourself with is your prize." The creature pointed to the portal.

I looked back again and stared into the swirling, purple vortex. This could all be over. All I had to do was step into the portal, and this would be done. That would be the end of the Planet of Shadows. I could go home ... But I couldn't. I'd been through too much; I couldn't walk away from this now. I had to see this through. I had to know why this happened. What was the point of anything that happened? This creature abducted us all for some kind of experiment, and I deserved answers.

"I can't go back," I said.

"Excuse me?" the creature growled.

"I can't go back until I know why. Why did you do it? After all this, I think I deserve to know why. Why did you take us from our worlds? Why did you bring us here? Why only two creatures from each planet? Why one male and one female? Why only humanoid creatures? Why do we all speak the same language? Why—"

The creature cut me off with a cry that sounded partially like the roar of a lion and partially like the scream of a madman.

"You will return to your world with no further questions," it demanded. "You're lucky I haven't killed you for your irritancy. Take your prize and leave."

I thought for a second. "Why haven't you killed me?"

The creature said nothing.

"You claim that The Third Event killed everyone on the planet. You want us dead, but you won't do it yourself. You could; I saw what you did with those shadows before. But you won't. Why?"

It remained silent.

"You're afraid of me, aren't you? You're afraid of all of us."

"That's preposterous."

"But it's true, isn't it? You can't kill me with an Event, you can't hide behind an experiment; if you want me dead, you have to fight me, but you won't because you're afraid you'll lose."

"You speak of matters far beyond your ken, human." The creature pointed to the purple portal. "Leave!"

I stepped toward the shadowy monster. "I won't."

It raised a hand, collecting the shadows into a towering wall. Then it pushed the wall toward me, and the wall pushed me toward the portal. I detached both my arms, sending two long-range punches to the creature's face. This managed to daze it, and the wall disappeared.

Calling back my arms, I ran toward the creature, but it quickly regained its focus and materialized another wall, this time with tentacles that latched onto my arms, restraining them.

The wall was pushing me back into the portal. I tried using my flight ability to escape, but the shadow tentacles were holding me back. I couldn't fly away, but maybe my thrusters were stronger than this wall; maybe I could use them to push against it.

I tried; I really did. I fully exerted all my strength, but the wall was stronger, and I was pushed into the portal. But before I was gone, before I crossed over into whatever was on the other side, I heard the creature say a few more words: "He's gone. It's over. Time to regroup with the others and present my data. Then we shall truly have nothing to fear."

And after that, I heard nothing more. I floated in an empty space, filled with vibrant blues, reds, and purples. The colour was splashed about, like ink blots on white paper. And then I bounced. Off of what, I don't know, but I flew through the air, bouncing up and down, left and right, over and under, in and out, everywhere.

Just before the vomit could escape my mouth, I stopped bouncing. Now I was trapped in a two-dimensional plain. How did I know it was two-dimensional? Because I could only see in two directions: forward and backward. There was no in-between. For a moment, I just floated there, in an endless, colourful, two-dimensional space. And then I cracked.

Like a glass window, I shattered. My shards, the pieces of my body, floated away from each other, and then they floated back toward each other. Away. Toward. Like a yo-yo. It didn't hurt, but I could feel every part of my body— where they were, where they were going, and how long it would take for them to get there. Everything. I saw my foot float by, and then my hand, and then my ear. None of this hurt; it was almost peaceful. But then I peered into my own eye.

One eye crossed the path of the other eye, and they stared into each other. Imagine looking into one of your eyes with the other. Can you imagine what you'd see? It's difficult, isn't it? Count yourself lucky that you can't see yourself through your own eyes, reflected again, and again, and again, and again. Over, and over, and over, and over in an endless loop, like a mirror reflecting another mirror. If my brain weren't cybernetically enhanced, I might not have been able to take it.

Luckily, this didn't last forever. I was suddenly reassembled and the third dimension returned, and with it, something new: gravity. I fell, but stacks of floating rocks assembled to hold up my feet. They appeared only when needed, gathering underneath my feet after every step. The rocks were also slightly delayed, so they were quite literally catching my falls, rather than me just walking across them. But then they stopped coming, and I really did fall.

While I plummeted, the colour around me was stripped away, uncovering the pure black that lay underneath. And as the colour was stripped, so too was my skin. It peeled off of me, revealing all the circuitry in my body.

In the distance, a small pool of water appeared, and as I fell toward it, it grew larger. But I wasn't plunged into it; I stopped falling just inches above the water. It gave me time to look at myself, at my reflection. No skin, no walls; all that remained was the truth. I was made of metal. My eyes were mere green lights. My body was full of pulleys and gears and flashing lights. I've been called robotic before, but it wasn't until now that I truly saw what everyone else had seen in me all along. And then I was shot upward into the air.

My skin returned, as did the blues, reds, and purples. I rocketed into the sky until I landed on the stony hand of a giant. The giant was so large that I could only see its head. The rest of its body was obscured in the surrounding colour. Its face was a simple skull made of rock, and it looked at me; it looked into me, deep within. It wasn't pleased. Its hand moved, and I fell again.

This time, my skin remained, but the surrounding colour still ripped away. In the distance, instead of a pool of water, I saw a street. A street with houses, streetlights, and birds. It was the same street I'd found that golden ring on ... all that time ago.

A low-pitched scream filled my ears. The closer I fell to the street, the higher the pitch became, until it stopped, and I hit the pavement hard.

The last thing I saw was the ring wrapped around my finger, the same golden ring that had brought me to the Planet of Shadows and then disappeared, never to be seen again. Why choose now to return?

The ring flashed three times with a red light, and I blacked out.

Chapter 23

The wind blew, lifting me out of my slumber. I pushed myself off the ground and stood. Immediately, I took a battle stance, expecting something life-threatening to happen, but then I realized ... this wasn't the Planet of Shadows. There were no endless deserts with burrowing dragon creatures, there were no insects whose swarms could decapitate you, and there were no snowy tundras that were hotter than words could describe. There were just roads made of tar, buildings made of concrete, and regular weather patterns.

"I'm home," I muttered. "It's over."

I walked down the suburban streets, on my way back to my house. But the longer I walked, the more I realized that something was wrong. It was quiet, way too quiet for the suburbs. Where is everyone? There were no people, no cars, nothing. What happened?

I stopped walking when I heard a crunching sound. Lifting my foot, I realized I had stepped on some bones.

They looked like a bird's skeleton. Come to think of it, I hadn't seen any birds either. What if ...? Oh no.

My walk turned into a run, and I quickly made it to my house. The front door was on the ground, detached from its hinges. I entered and dropped to my knees. Everything had been destroyed—the furniture, the doors and windows—and there were skeletons on the floor. Human skeletons.

I wiped tears from my eyes and ran back outside. Taking to the air, I flew up to the highest building I could find and looked out at the world. It was true; everyone was gone. No people, no animals. How did this happen?

I took to the air again and grounded myself at a small park full of dead trees.

What am I going to do? Everyone's gone, dead. Is the whole planet like this? This is just like what that woman said—Sandy. She said that when she went to her alien companion's planet, everyone was dead—all life, gone. Did someone do this? Did an alien race invade Earth while I was gone? ... I'm going to die. I can't run an entire planet on my own. Who will maintain the water pipes? Who will gather food? Who will warn me if a hurricane approaches? This is it. My reward for surviving the Planet of Shadows is to die in the ruins of my old life.

I sat on the grassy ground. A glint caught my eye—the golden ring. It was still wrapped around my finger, and the brown leather bracelet was still around my wrist. I couldn't pretend that none of it happened; the proof was on my hand. I removed the ring and bracelet, foolishly hoping that everything would magically be fixed once I did, but nothing changed. The bracelet was just a bracelet, and the ring was just a ring, the ring that ruined my life.

I chucked the bracelet away, and then I threw the ring as far as I could, but it didn't get very far at all. Someone caught it in midair.

"I think I'll hold on to this, if you don't mind," said the old man, slipping the ring into a pocket on his white lab coat.

I took a good look at him. He had grey hair and a moustache, a wooden walking stick, and he was quite wrinkly as well. My robotic brain placed a grey circle around him, captioned: "Unknown".

"Oh, my god," I breathed. "Another human being. Not everyone is dead."

"Oh, no, I'm not human," said the man, sitting on the ground next to me.

"What do you mean you're not human? You look human, and you're on Earth."

"That's quite true. But all the same, I'm not human, not in the way you'd expect anyway."

"So, you're an alien?"

"Not quintessentially."

I looked down, confused by what he'd said.

"What's the matter, Charles?" he asked me.

"How do you know my name?"

"Honestly, lad, you haven't even answered my question before you've come up with your own."

I hesitated. "Everyone's dead. Everyone on the Planet of Shadows and everyone here."

"Aye, I'm afraid so."

I looked at him suspiciously.

"No, I didn't do it," he said before I even had the chance to wonder. He bit his lip. "I'm sorry."

I looked down.

"You see," he continued, "I don't believe your sorrow stems solely from the fact that everyone is gone or even from your traumatic time on the Planet of Shadows. I think it stems from the fact that you now feel lost. A lot has happened to you, and you are unsure of what to do."

"Who are you?"

"Professor Thomas. I would shake your hand, but I know you're not too keen on that."

"How do you know so much about me?"

"Because he's been watching you." A woman stole Professor Thomas's turn to speak. "He travels the multiverse, watching loads of different people, so he knows a lot of things."

The woman, approaching from behind, was dressed all in black. Her skin was light, but in contrast, her veins were extremely dark, almost like ink. Her hair was short, black, and a little messy. She seemed fully bereft of any colour. Even her eyes were completely colourless. My mind placed a red circle around her, captioned:

"Caution". In reaction to this, I stood up and got ready to defend.

"Relax," she said. "I'm not going to hurt you."

I didn't let up my stance.

"Charles," said the professor, "this is Sarah, who is so rudely interrupting at the moment." He looked at her.

"Whatever," she said. "We don't have time for this. Just explain it to him, and let's go."

"Perhaps, Ms. Pickaro, it would be best for you to leave this part to me."

She rolled her eyes and looked at me. "Look, you know what a shadow-dweller is, yeah?"

"Um, sort of," I said.

"You must know how dangerous they are. They've been travelling throughout the multiverse, from dimension to dimension, destroying people's lives, world by world. It looks like they've already gotten to your world, and it sucks; trust me, I know. But now they're gathering in Dimension-005, and we need to go quickly. We need you to help us stop them."

"What are you talking about?" I asked. "Who's *we*, and what's Dimension-005?"

"Ms. Pickaro, I think you should return to the ship," said Professor Thomas. "Go check on Pete for me. I don't want him messing up one of those bloody potions again. It took him ages to find an antidote for those rabbit tails the last time. Oh, and tell Alex to get his suit ready. I think that is something young Mr. McCoy here would like to see.”

“‘Alex’?” the woman smirked. “You mean *Scar*?”

“I do not subscribe to the use of that name.”

She sighed. “Fine, but hurry up. We don’t have all day.” She walked away and entered a spaceship I hadn’t noticed until now. It had a sleek white design with minimal windows, a door on the side, and there were short wings and flaps all around it.

“There’s someone named Alex in there?” I asked the professor, pointing to the spaceship.

“Ah, yes. It was foretold by that scrappy time traveller that you would meet Alex, wasn’t it?”

“You know Tom?”

He looked at me, studying my face. “Yes and no. I’ve never actually met him.”

I was beyond confused. “What is going on? Who are you?”

“As much as I hate to admit it, Sarah is right. I’ll have to explain the specifics at a later time, I’m afraid. For now, you’ll follow me into my ship.”

“You just assume that I’ll go with you?”

“It’s not an assumption; I know you will.”

“How?”

“The same way I know the reason why I want you to come.”

“What’s the reason?”

I looked at him, fixated on the “Unknown” caption.

"You're a smart lad," he said. "Why do you think a man such as I would require your assistance in dealing with the threat of the shadow-dwellers?"

I pondered this question. The only reason he would specifically need me is if I could do something that no one else could, right? So, what makes me different?

"Is it because I'm a cyborg?" I wondered. "That makes me unique."

"I wouldn't be so sure." He showed me his arm after tapping it with his finger. Flashing lights appeared underneath his skin, and I could hear the hum of electronics.

"You have cybernetic enhancements, too?"

He smiled. "You and I are not too different, Mr. McCoy. There was a time in my life when I needed these enhancements just as a time came in your life when you needed yours. But that is not why I need your help."

"Then why? What makes me different?"

"Not *what, because.*"

"I don't understand."

"I need you *because* you are different, Charles. You see, throughout your exploits on the Planet of Shadows, I think you've learned quite an invaluable lesson."

"What lesson?"

"That greatness stems from abnormality. Do you think the person who created the first computer was considered normal? Do you think he could easily fit in with others? What about the lass who created the slatherus?"

"The what?"

He paused. "Sorry, wrong world. It's a device for creating and controlling planets; just forget I said anything. My point is, great ideas don't come from normal people, they come from those of us who are strange, insane, weird, and reclusive. Those are the people who push the rest of us forward."

"So you need me because I'm weird?"

"Not quintessentially." He stood up and looked at his spaceship in the distance. "The reason I want you to join me, and the reason I know you ultimately will, is because you, Mr. McCoy, are just beginning to understand that it's okay to be weird. And that knowledge is the most powerful thing I have ever come across in all the multiverse."

Afterword

This book was certainly a fun one to go back to. I was seventeen when I wrote the original draft of *Planet of Shadows*, and I remember having two goals: I wanted to write a book with an autistic protagonist, and I wanted to really let loose with my creativity and think up as many different types of people, practices, and perspectives as I could.

I've been writing since I was very young, and a lot of the adults around me used to say that I was very creative for writing fiction. But I personally never found it to be all that creative. I have a very hard definition of what I consider to be creative, and it's a little difficult to explain. To me, it's like the difference between a painter who paints fantasy worlds so fantastical that they could never exist in reality, and a painter who paints realism. Both are impressive skills, but one requires more creativity than the other. And I don't mean that as a bad thing at all; art is a creative medium, and so every work of art—be it visual, musical, written, or what have you—will involve a bit of creativity. I just don't think that every good work of art is automatically *creative* just for being in a creative medium. But I admit, my definition of the word is probably quite askew. Perhaps I'm conflating it with the word *imaginative*.

Among my own writing, I consider *Planet of Shadows* to be my most creative. I got to invent so many creatures and people; I got to imagine how they would act and what sorts of lives they would lead. That made it really fun for me to write.

This book also ended up having a lot to do with mental health. When writing Charles, I drew on a lot of my own experiences as an autistic person, as well as the experiences of autistic people I'd met while being schooled in ASD classes. Charles being asked by his teacher if he knew what time it was in the beginning of the book is something that happened to me in real life, and like Charles, I didn't pick up on the sarcasm. Charles's interest in computers comes from that being a common interest among many of my autistic peers, though it wasn't an interest I personally shared.

I also made sure not to treat autism as a problem here. It's just a difference. The only reason autism is considered a disorder is because the world is designed for allistic people, not autistic people. But both allism and autism have their strengths and weaknesses. I've always thought of it like running on different operating systems. Maybe you run on Windows, maybe you run on macOS. Neither is better or worse than the other; they're just different, with their own strengths and weaknesses. I made sure to showcase in this book some of the weaknesses of autism, such as Charles's difficulty in understanding sarcasm; and some of the strengths of autism, such as Charles's ability to problem-solve. And I also showcased some of the strengths of allism, such as Ruby's more intuitive ability to read a person's emotional state; and some of the weaknesses of allism, such as Angela having difficulty connecting with all the wildly different people on the Planet of Shadows. Of course, these examples of autism and allism aren't all-encompassing. The workings of the human mind are complex, after all. But hopefully, I was able to show that, though they have their differences, neither is the better one. They are both equally different.

I also got to explore psychosis and general breaks in reality for this book. I remember when I was seventeen and writing the first draft, I wanted Stryx to have schizophrenia because the media often depicts that as something that can make a character evil (the same way media often depicts Dissociative Identity Disorder, Antisocial Personality Disorder and psychopathy, and other things of that sort as a cause for why a person is evil). I wanted to have a character with schizophrenia who wasn't evil in any way. Stryx is someone who protects people, and incidentally, he's not really aware that he is schizophrenic, so it's just part of who he is. And then there was the cintin water, and Charles's "descent into madness," as it were. I feel I got to explore addiction and psychosis in a really interesting way here, and I hoped to create a situation where the reader is also wondering what is real and what isn't, and whether Charles as a narrator is all that reliable.

And speaking of that, one thing I did change while writing this revised version of *Planet of Shadows* was how I wrote Charles's narration. Something that is excellent about books is their ability to put you into the mind of a character and really let you experience things through their eyes. I did this in *Sarah*, where everything was described as either light or dark because Sarah is colour-blind, and common things are described as alien shapes because she has very little experience with being sighted, and thus, cannot accurately describe what things look like. So for Charles, this was an opportunity to show an example of what it's like to be autistic and to think autistically. I often described the visual actions a character was doing rather than describing what those actions meant. For example, I might say a character just "smiled" rather than "smiled slyly". I made a lot of the body language in the book ambiguous to represent what it would be like to have trouble interpreting that, to see people making expressions and gestures but not always understanding what they mean. And for any allistic people reading this book, I invented some body language that doesn't exist in human societies for the people on the Planet of Shadows to use (such as Skylar's tendency to pull on his droopy ears), and I made those ambiguous, too. So whether you are autistic or allistic, there is body language in this book that you probably had difficulty interpreting, and that is a little taste of what Charles's form of autism feels like.

Something I really enjoy about this book is all the things you get to experience on the Planet of Shadows. Some of my favourites were the drillmite, the twitchflies, the Cave of Xania; and in terms of people, I love the idea of Doctor Trevor and Cassie, a highly advanced doctor and assistant who take the form of children because they age backward. I hope you were able to have a few particularly memorable experiences on the Planet of Shadows as well.

And with that, I think it's time to wrap this up. Next is the final *Tales of the Multiverse* book, *The Mysterious Four*, the book that eighteen-year-old me contributed to this series. But before then, thank you for reading this book. I hope you enjoyed it, and I hope you'll join me again for the next one. See you there.

- R. J. F., July 2023

247